SKIN CAGE

NICO LAESER

NICO LAESER

Copyright © 2015 by Jennifer Laeser
All rights reserved. This book or any portion thereof may not be reproduced or used in any manner whatsoever without the express written permission of the publisher except for the use of brief quotations in a book review.

Cover design by Nico Laeser

Editing by Kelly Hartigan (XterraWeb)
editing.xterraweb.com

NicoLaeser@gmail.com

ISBN-13: 978-1506188225
ISBN-10: 1506188222

For Jennifer

I

CHAPTER 1

I am Daniel

In my dream, she is dressed in her white uniform, with a burgundy cardigan over top. Her hair is styled almost like a movie star from the fifties, and if the world suddenly became black and white, she would be indiscernible from any of the leading ladies in any of the old movies that play on daytime television.

Sunlight floods through the window in a wide beam and shines through the side of her right eye, as she sits in her chair, gazing thoughtfully off into the corner of the room. I can see the clear convex cornea of her eye and behind it, the intricate pattern of her iris, a beautiful and delicate flower encased and preserved in resin. The petals of the flower surrounding the black pupil are all the colors of autumn, flecks of green, amber, and every shade of brown. As I stare into her eyes, I feel the effects of inertia as a familiar gravity begins pulling me in toward her, and my heart and stomach tense in preparation, anticipating free-fall.

Her unpainted lips appear soft and are the subtle pink color of Jersey Lilies, contrasting the pale skin of her face, which appears almost white when illuminated by the sun. The soft peach fuzz that blurs and softens the edges is highlighted as a white haze, from the base of her slender neck, to behind her ear. I am envious of the warm and gentle breeze that caresses the topography of her bare skin, her perfect skin, undamaged by the sun and rarely exposed to it directly because she spends her days here, with me.

My name is Daniel. She calls me Danny, and although I cringe inside when anyone calls me Danny, I can't tell her this. I am in love with her.

I am around six feet tall, and in my mind, of athletic build. My voice is deep and gravelly and this is the voice that narrates my thoughts and dreams, and it is with this inner voice that I tell her every day that I love her, though I can't say it to her out loud.

***

I awake from the dream, and the room seems dim in contrast to the vivid colors of the dream. I'm moving down the hallway, toward my bedroom, when I see her. Her autumn eyes light up, and the smile I adore spreads across her soft heart-shaped face, held in place by a slender neck, housed in the white collar of her uniform and framed by the same burgundy cardigan from my dream.

I follow the slim arms of the cardigan down to her delicate wrists and tender hands that curl around the handles of the wheelchair that contains *him*, the pathetic, useless mass, the dormant obstacle that has prevented me from ever having the chance to tell her how I feel. His twisted, gape-mouthed face frames eyes that I recognize.

She points at me and says, "Look, Danny, who's that handsome guy?"

I see her burgundy arm and slender finger, outstretched over my shoulder, pointing back at the retard. The full-size, badly sculpted clay model of a man is slumped in the wheelchair, and staring back at me, but it is not *my* reflection that I see in the mirror.

Danny is my prison, my skin cage.

I am his prisoner. I am Daniel.

CHAPTER 2

I am her diary

I lie awake in my bed, studying the decorative moulding that circles the hanging chandelier. The sunlight bounces off the pendant glass, creating long drawn out patterns on the otherwise plain white ceiling. I know, by the position of the shadows and reflections, that I still have over an hour before Cassie and Anna come to get me, and all I can do is wait.

I hate waking up early. I try to force myself to fall back asleep but without success. My mouth seems dry, more so than usual, and there is an itch on my body somewhere, but I'm not sure exactly where. I go to one of the places that I usually go to in my mind, when I have time to kill.

I am sitting outside a hut, fashioned from tall lengths of thick bamboo, staked into the arid dirt and lashed together with strips of the green outer skin from the bamboo. Its roof is made from layered palm leaves as opposed to some of the other huts in the village that have switched to corrugated metal. In front of me sits a boy of indiscernible age, whose name is unpronounceable in English. Our conversation is limited to head and hand gestures, and I copy his movements. We each have a bone handle knife and shape strips of hard bamboo into twelve-inch skewers, much like the barbecue skewers that you can buy in any supermarket back home.

Once we have around forty or so skewers each, we set them aside, and he places the weeds that we collected earlier from the rainforest on the ground between us. It is a type of wild-growing weed that resembles a milk thistle. He cuts the flower part off two of them and hands one to me. He makes eye contact briefly to make sure that I am watching, then he pulls at the cotton-like material, and I mimic his actions. He cuts the heads off all the weeds and places them before me, and I repeat the process with each.

At the end of this process, we have a fist-size ball of fibrous white fluff, and he places a rock on top of it to stop it from blowing away in the blistering hot breeze. He takes the stems of the weed and peels each like a banana, creating long thin green strands and gestures for me to do the same. He takes his knife and puts a small cut into the non-pointed end of one of the skewers before taking a piece of the cobweb-like fluff and pulling it into a ten-inch length. He takes one of the long green strings and slides it into the cut in the end of the skewer, then begins to wrap the fluff and string around the end of the skewer. Every couple of turns, he pulls at the fluff. He ties off the string and cuts off the excess. He takes the completed dart and pushes it into the long bamboo tube before raising it to his lips. He exhales with great force into the mouthpiece. The sound of rushing air is followed by a miniature thud as the dart sticks deep into a cardboard box that reads, "Christian missionaries: relief support."

***

I hear talking and realize that I have been moved from my bed to my chair and have completely missed the morning's cleaning ritual and the treating of my bedsores.

"Do you need anything else, Cass?" Anna touches Cassie's arm and smiles, revealing the dark pink vertical lines carved into the black-brown skin, stretched over her rounded left cheek.

As a boy, I failed to appreciate the power of such a simple gesture: instead, I would find myself staring with morbid curiosity at her scars, which ironically, seemed to appear only when she smiled fully.

"I don't need anything else right now; thanks, I'll take it from here," Cassie says.

"Would you like some coffee?" Anna says over her shoulder as she leaves the room.

From over *my* shoulder, Cassie says, "That would be lovely; thanks, Anna," and we follow her out.

As we exit the room, I make a great effort to keep my eyes pinned right or closed, so as to avoid the oversized mirror at the end of the hallway that serves as a crushing daily reminder of the inaccuracy of my self-image.

We move down toward the day room, passing ornate frames housing painted representations of my ancestors, three-quarter-turned figures, each with the same stern glare of self-importance. The centerline, where the textured filigree wall coverings above meet the wood paneling below, serves as the line of symmetry between the frames of the paintings and the frames that make up the relief detail in the wood paneling. The mahogany wood panel wainscoting continues for the lower four feet of almost every wall in the house, including the curved staircase. The same color runs through the wood floor that is polished to a high luster, reflecting an upside-down and slightly darker version of the house interior.

I let myself become entranced by the sound of Cassie's heels on the wood floor and by the distant sound of Anna's flat shoes slapping her feet as she lifts each leg, her shoes squeaking at every turn and becoming gradually quieter with the *clip-slap* of each step.

Once in the day room, Cassie begins my morning exercises, starting with my legs, one at a time, bending and stretching them at the knee; she begins rolling and stretching my ankle as she braces my left leg on top of her bended knee, before doing the same with my right.

She stands up and takes one of my arms. Out of my peripheral vision, I can see her extending and contracting the arm at the elbow, then rolling the ball joint of the shoulder. She pulls her chair close to mine and sits down, taking one of my hands and rolling it at the wrist, before interlocking her fingers with mine and continuing the exercise. I cannot feel her hand in mine, but sometimes it almost seems like I can. I suppose that this is my mind attempting to simulate the sensation, in response to the received visual information. I know that the *feeling* is not real, but this is still my favorite part of the morning.

Cassie repositions my chair by the table next to the window and moves her chair opposite mine.

Anna walks into view with steaming coffee and sets the cup down on the table. "There you go, my dear."

"You are an angel." Cassie takes Anna's hand in both of hers, and by contrast, they look black and white.

"How is that no-good boyfriend of yours?" Anna asks, adding her other hand to the pile.

"Still no good, but no longer my boyfriend," Cassie replies.

"Probably for the best. Some men just don't know how to behave," Anna says.

Cassie pulls back the corners of her mouth in a pseudo smile. "He's been calling me, leaving messages, saying he's sorry, that it meant nothing, and that he wants to talk."

"That boy is not good enough for you, Cass, actions speak louder than words," Anna says and moves her hand to Cassie's shoulder.

Cassie nods. "He said that it was a simple mistake. Picking up salt instead of sugar at a diner is a simple mistake; picking up another woman instead of your girlfriend at the bar—well we both know what they did—that's *not* a simple mistake."

Anna stands there, shaking her head. "You need to find yourself a nice church-going boy."

"I wasn't even looking for a boyfriend; he just appeared out of nowhere one day and wouldn't take no for an answer. He was persistent and he brought me flowers. I figured that he couldn't be that bad if he was willing to wait more than two months until I would even agree to meet him for coffee," Cassie says.

"You're not thinking of giving him another chance, are you?" Anna asks.

"No way, I could never be with anyone that thinks so little of me," Cassie replies.

Anna smiles and gently squeezes the hand on Cassie's shoulder. "Mr. Right will come along one day." She takes back her hands. "I'll leave you and Danny to it. Let me know if you need anything else."

"Thanks, Anna, I think we have everything we need," Cassie says.

Anna exits my field of view.

Cassie's phone vibrates and travels slowly across the table. She looks at it, rolls her eyes, and touches the screen. It stops vibrating and she leaves it on the table.

"Sorry, Danny, that rotten liar does not deserve any more of my time, or yours." She smiles and looks me in the eyes. "You know, when I was living in the foster home with Brian, I sent off for a 'build your own lie detector kit.' I waited for two weeks until it came and then spent almost three hours putting it together before testing it on Brian."

She raises the steaming cup to her lips and winces before setting it back on the table, "I asked a few simple control questions to test it out and then got down to the reason that I had ordered it in the first place: 'did you, Brian, take and read my diary?' I asked. He denied it emphatically and the lie detector lit up. I yelled at him, calling him a liar, and he broke down and confessed, saying that there was nothing interesting in it anyway. After he promised to never touch my things again, cross his heart and hope to die and all that, he skulked out of my room, and I hooked myself up to the contraption. 'Am I the smartest, most brilliant person in the world?' I asked and answered, 'yes,' and it lit up again. I stuck out my tongue at the machine and returned to the simple control questions that I'd asked of Brian. 'Is my name Cassandra?' I asked and answered, 'yes,' and it lit up again. At the time I wondered if I'd wired it wrong, but more likely, it was just a kid's novelty kit that didn't actually work." She purses her perfect lips and blows steam across the surface of her coffee cup before taking a sip.

"At first, I was angry about being duped by the makers of the kit, but over time, whenever Brian would fail to own up to something that I knew he'd done, I would just threaten to pull out the lie detector, and he would own up to it, all in a huff. His first response was always to lie though, about whatever it was, and if I didn't have the lie detector, which Brian thought of as an infallible tattletale, then I'm pretty sure that he would never have told the truth." She shakes her head and sighs. "Some people don't deserve the benefit of the doubt and will only tell the truth if they have no other option. The best thing to do with people like that is to cut them out of your life completely."

Cassie reaches into her bag and pulls out the book that she has been reading to me. "Let's get back to a man whose stories *are* worth listening to—Mr. Tolkien," she says, opens the book to the page she has bookmarked, and begins to read.

CHAPTER 3

I am worm food

My parents are Robert and Hilary Stockholm. My father was the sole heir to the fortune of Montgomery Stockholm, my grandfather. My mother spent most of her life traveling the poorest parts of the globe, helping under-privileged communities. Her family was also wealthy and took it upon themselves to heal the world one fundraiser or Christian school at a time. My parents met at one of the fundraisers for starving kids in Africa. These gatherings were by invitation only and were usually made up of the incredibly rich, and ironically, most self-absorbed people. To my mother's credit, she is a second-generation do-gooder. Her childhood was spent living among the people that her parents were trying to help, and as a result, she was denied the rich brat upbringing that the child of such a wealthy family is usually accustomed; instead, she was subjected to a lot of the same hardships as the poor wasteland dwellers of the various third-world countries they frequented.

My mother had continued the crusade to help the less fortunate, and much like her, as a child, I had been dragged along. I was proud of what my parents were trying to accomplish, but at the same time, I felt like my needs were never really taken into account. My summers were spent in one dusty, blistering hot wasteland or another, surrounded by various shades of skeletal kids with bloated bellies and mouths containing sporadic yellowed teeth. In spite of my family's wealth, I, like little Hilary, was to spend my summers in large tents or huts made from bamboo and leaves or corrugated steel and junk.

In a, 'what I did during summer,' essay, I wrote instead, a story of a child whose mother and father were both firefighters. The child was brought along to watch with pride as his mother and father rushed into burning buildings, fighting back the flames to rescue blackened, choking people, before extinguishing the fires to give the people back their homes and cherished items. In my story, the child suffered from the accumulated effects of smoke inhalation, and over time, the flames, blistering heat, and tortured, twisted faces of the people trapped in the blackness, fueled recurring nightmares that replaced adoration and pride with fear and resentment.

I was not starving or dying of malaria, but I was living in squalor and surrounded by pain, misery, and death, while all the other kids from my school were off skiing in the Alps or sunbathing on a private beach somewhere.

Upon returning to school, the other kids would talk about frivolous shopping sprees in Paris or high-class cruise vacations with a stay at some tropical destination. They would show each other what they had brought back, an expensive designer watch or sunglasses or rare, dead-animal-skin jacket. The only thing I would have in common with the other kids was a tan, minus the pale skin in the shape of ski goggles.

What I brought back from one of my summer vacations was something that would last much longer, and would affect me more profoundly, than any expensive surrogate for parental attention.

After a couple months stint helping to build a Christian school or install an irrigation system in one or another barren landscape, something came with us on the plane—a hijacker. The hijacker passed through airport security undetected and followed us back home, where it would take only one hostage, before beginning a series of attacks that would destroy my world forever. The hijacker was a tapeworm.

Tapeworm larvae somehow found its way to my brain and would stay there, housed in a cyst, and feed off my brain unnoticed for years, until one day, during track and in full sprint, I collapsed mid-run. I was fifteen years old.

It felt, for a second, like trying to run across a lake; the momentum carried me forward as I lost control of my legs, and gravity did the rest. My body went limp, and I slammed hard to the track.

I opened my eyes to a bright sun, fast moving silhouettes, and a high-pitched squeal inside my head. People moved around frantically, and my head felt like someone had smashed it open with a hammer. The sunlight and the blaring siren of the ambulance served to amplify the splitting pain in my head, which was so excruciating that I failed to realize that it was the *only* thing that I could still feel.

CHAPTER 4

I am the shorn lamb

It is the first of the month, or thereabouts. I know this because my chair is covered with a thin veil of plastic that makes a shushing, rustling sound when I'm lowered into it. I listen to the rustle of the plastic as the wheels rub against it on our way to the day room.

I open my eyes when we come to a stop, parked in front of the day room window. The windows are full height and stretch the full length of the day room, separated by floor-to-ceiling columns every twelve feet or so, and each section between is split by a large cross of ornate framework, housing the four individual panes of glass. There is warmth that I feel on my face, but I attribute this to nostalgia, rather than the actual warmth of the morning sun that pours through the glass.

Anna places the leather case on the table, unzips and opens it, revealing the electric hair shears and all of the accessories, of which, she will only use one—the quarter-inch guard. She attaches the guard and plugs the long cord into the wall socket on the face of the nearest column, before draping another light blue plastic veil over my body and disappearing behind me.

The growling buzz orbits my senses as the sun highlights a haze of half-inch lines that drift down slowly in front of me. I close my eyes and ignore the psychosomatic itch that begins to crawl and spread over my upper body.

I am unsure as to which is the greater lie: the image in the mirror that reflects a contorted immobile stranger, or the self-image I maintain in my mind of a clean-shaven, well-groomed man, closely resembling a younger version of my father. I know it is the latter, which plays the leading role in almost all of my thoughts and dreams.

I was never allowed the opportunity to cut my own facial hair. I remember, when I was a child, staring up at my father shaving carefully in front of the bathroom mirror. I would stand next to him, barely up to his elbow, idolizing him and emulating his movements with the back of my toothbrush.

The last time I watched my father shave, I was around nine years old. He sliced his cheek with the razor, deep enough to make him drop the razor into the sink and curse.

"You didn't hear me say that." My father had winked at me and pressed a wad of tissue that immediately blotted red against his cheek.

"No Dad," I replied with a smirk, knowing that he was referring to the curse word.

"I nicked myself pretty good there," he said, viewing his reflection out of the corner of his eye and dabbing at the cut with fresh tissue.

When he moved his hand away, I could see the red line splitting swollen pink skin. "You look like Aunt Anna," I said.

My father shot a disapproving glance in my direction and shushed me. "Don't you say that in front of Anna."

"Why not?" I asked.

"Some things are better left alone. Your Aunt Anna's scars are one of those things," he said in a hushed but firm tone.

I continued to stare at my father. "I don't understand."

My father took a seat on the edge of the bathtub and sighed through his nose. "You know that Grandma Jane used to visit poor countries to help people, just like your mother and I do now, right?"

I nodded in response.

"Well," he stopped and let out the air from his lungs, but not the words.

I waited patiently for him to reassemble his thoughts and continue.

"You know that Grandma Jane rescued Anna from one of those places when Anna was just a little girl?" he asked rhetorically, to which I nodded.

"Well, there were people that lived in Anna's village who wanted to hurt her," my father said.

"Why?" I asked.

My father shuffled uncomfortably. "They thought that Anna and her sister were witches."

"They thought Mom was a witch too?" I asked.

"Your mom? No. Anna had another sister, before your grandma took her in." My father stared at the floor.

It was obvious to me from an early age that Anna was not a blood relative, but up until then, I was unaware that she had another sister. "What happened to her sister?"

"Your grandma wasn't able to save her in time," he replied through his hand as he rubbed at his freshly shaved jaw.

"Did they hurt her?" I asked.

My father seemed to wake from a daydream in apparent shock to my question and took a second to process it.

"Yes." He nodded. "They did."

"Where is she now?" I asked.

"She's with Grandma Jane," he replied.

"In heaven?"

My father nodded slowly with that same forced, straight-line smile that usually meant he was uncomfortable or unsure. He never talked to me again about Anna's scars, and I would have to wait impatiently for just over three years to learn the rest of the horrific story from my mother.

***

I open my eyes to the silhouette of Anna brushing the hair from my face and neck. She turns my chair away from the window, and as my eyes adjust to the relatively dark day room, Anna's smiling face appears.

"Well, don't you look handsome, Danny," she says.

CHAPTER 5

I am Medusa

The headaches come and go. Sometimes they are mild, and sometimes they are worse than anything I had ever felt before, when I could still feel anything at all. My senses that remain are sight, smell, and hearing, and other than smell, all of these senses are obscured or distorted by the pain that sears and burns through my brain during one of my headaches.

My sensitivity to light and noise become intolerable, and if I can, I close my eyes tight. This is not always possible, as even my eyes sometimes require immense persuasion before they will obey my request. The subtle sounds of the machines and apparatus that work around me, to keep me breathing, fed, and whatever else, become loud like pistons, pile drivers, and jackhammers. It feels like I am transported at once to the interior of a demolition site, with all the work lights flooding through the open windows, blinding me, as the building is smashed down around me with a thunderous cracking and rumbling.

About two years after I collapsed and was permanently paralyzed, I was sitting in my chair, and one of my headaches began like microphone feedback. The squealing evolved quickly into a localized pain and then immense pressure, like someone was pushing down on my head with great force, crushing and grinding my skull into the vertebrae of my neck. The pain was incredible, and I could not call out for help or beg for medication. It was unbearable torture. Like a trapped animal that chews through its own leg to escape a trap, I somehow chewed myself free.

I was standing, looking at a much darker version of the day room. All of the furniture and objects in the room were represented in varying shades of blue. I turned and stared at the person-shaped mass in a seated position, glowing like the ghosted image that lingers in front of your eyes after staring at a bright light. It was my body, and I was no longer trapped inside it. I thought that I had died.

The closer I came to objects, the clearer and more defined they became. I moved to the wall of the day room and toward the grid pattern that I knew to be the bookshelf. I had to move in close to view the words embossed on the spines, but I could not read the text on any of those that were not in three-dimensional relief. I placed my fingers on top of one of the books and tried to pull it from the shelf, but it didn't move. I tried to push and pull other objects—a vase containing fake flowers—but not even the flowers would budge, as if they, and everything else, had been turned to stone.

I made my way down the hall and out into the entranceway before continuing on into the kitchen. I saw another figure with the same primary color glow. I approached the figure that was stopped in mid-turn, holding a tray. I attempted to push the immovable objects on the tray and then leaned onto the tray itself, but nothing gave; everything was frozen solid.

I don't know how long I wandered around the house or if time can be used to describe the duration of my exploration. I moved through every room of the house that was not sealed off by a closed and immovable door.

When I returned to the day room where I had started, I studied the glowing figure in the chair, with light emanating from its mouth and eyes like the melting photographic negative of a bowling ball. I was expecting to feel yet another solid, unyielding mass, but was surprised as my hand passed through the figure. There was a wall of sound, screaming and pounding. I was back in my body, and the pain in my head returned at once, as if it had been turned on with a switch.

The pain lasted out the sunlight and then gradually faded back to a dull throb. This was the first time that I escaped my cage, but it would not be the last.

CHAPTER 6

I am not in love with my captor

I first heard the term, "Stockholm Syndrome," from Mr. Farley, an English professor at my high school. I had been sent to detention by the mathematics professor, Mr. Cornell, for almost three consecutive weeks following an incident in his class. He seemed to harbor a genuine loathing toward me, and this sentiment was more than reciprocated on my part.

The boy that sat next to me in Mr. Cornell's class was named John. John had become a good friend. Spending my summers away and out of touch made it difficult to retain friends, and John's parents had him signed up for a variety of classes during the summer to help him with his dyslexia, so we found ourselves in the same position when trying to maintain friendships and popularity.

John often had trouble reading the questions from the textbook, so I would read them to him aloud, so that he could get the words and numbers straight in his head. Mr. Cornell had accused John of cheating and said that I was giving him the answers.

"I'm trying to help him, he's dyslexic. I'm just reading out the questions," I had said in my defense.

"He's not dyslexic, he's an idiot, and you must think that I'm an idiot, if you expect me to believe such an asinine excuse, Mr. Stockholm," Mr. Cornell said.

"I don't expect you to believe anything, sir, and yes, I do think you're an idiot," I said without taking the time to adequately censor my thoughts.

Mr. Cornell's cheeks lit up like the taillights on a car, and the glint in his eyes, like that of a freshly honed knife blade, made me shuffle around in my seat. He rushed toward me and snatched me up by my shirt collar. He readjusted his grip as I squirmed, trapping some of my skin within his grasp as he dragged me out into the hall.

He slammed me hard into the wall, and in a hushed but stern tone, he said, "You just earned yourself a week in detention, you impudent little shit."

I was not a particularly gifted student, but up until this point, I was rarely referred to as disruptive, or singled out for punishment. I had flown under the radar, kept my mouth shut and head down, managing to remain undetected, surreptitiously cloaked by mediocrity.

Mr. Farley was an English professor who also ran a creative writing course held in the library after school. This was also where I was to spend my ongoing detention.

"You seem to be suffering from the syndrome of your namesake, Mr. Stockholm," Mr. Farley had said upon my appearance in detention for the second consecutive week.

"I don't know what you mean, sir," I said.

"Stockholm Syndrome," he said with raised intonation, posing it as a question.

My blank expression led to Mr. Farley elaborating on the subject.

"Stockholm Syndrome refers to people in captivity that begin to think positively of their captors," he said.

"I've never heard of it, sir," I replied.

"Maybe you should look into it, because if you are here in detention for a third week, then I will be expecting you to write an essay on it, and maybe you can include why it is that you keep finding yourself here, Mr. Stockholm," he said.

In August 1973, a man took four hostages during the robbery of a bank in Stockholm, Sweden. The perpetrator of the robbery kept four employees of the bank, three women and one man, hostage in the vault for 131 hours. During this time, the hostages began to exhibit empathy for their captor, refused assistance from government officials and began to view the police as an enemy. A psychiatric consultant named

Nils Bejerot attended the standoff and was the person responsible for the term Stockholm Syndrome.

I wrote a very detailed version of this in my essay that read like an excerpt from a poorly plagiarized Tom Clancy novel. As a footnote, I wrote that although I share my last name with a location in Sweden, I am not a sufferer of the aforementioned syndrome.

I went on to explain in writing why I had been sent to detention continuously since the initial incident, because I found it impossible to remain silent, while Mr. Cornell berated John and relegated him to the status of idiot, in what I viewed as an obvious attempt to instigate a rise out of me.

I wrote in my conclusion, "After calling my dyslexic friend an idiot, he raises an eyebrow and asks me if I have something to say, which I always do, the sentiment of which is the reason for my prolonged incarceration."

After reading my essay, Mr. Farley had asked me about the incident, and I had explained it in greater detail. A couple weeks later, both John and I were moved into a new math class, and John would receive extra help from the new teacher.

Mr. Farley had asked me if I wanted to attend his classes in creative writing after school since I now had free time upon being released from my "prolonged incarceration," and I did. He was a good teacher, and although I was not a particularly gifted writer, I developed a love for literature. What I had learned in his classes would be put to use on my family vacations to non-English speaking, poverty-stricken regions of the world, whether it was reading something that Mr. Farley had recommended, or writing about the trip and handing it in later as part of my, "What I did this summer" assignment, upon returning to school.

I found that over time, I did learn to think positively of Mr. Farley, but I didn't think of him as my captor; he was quite the opposite. He had allowed me the tools to escape captivity.

Years later, I would be revealed as my own antagonist. My true captor, my own body, would become my cell, with only two small windows for me to view the outside world.

Whenever I see my gape-mouth reflection, I think of him as my captor, though it was not Danny's fault or his intention to trap me inside; he is akin to the amber that seals a bug inside, preserving it for centuries.

I am the trapped bug, but unlike the bug, I was not fortunate enough to die.

CHAPTER 7

I am a good little bird

Cassie is not here today; I already know this as I lie in my bed staring at the chandelier sundial. I know this because I can hear the loud revving engine of a 1972 Ford Mustang as it pulls into the driveway. This is Marcus Salt's car; I know the sound of the engine, and I know that it is his because I listen to him brag about it on the phone, and for the last couple of years, whenever I hear that particular vehicle, he shows up instead of Cassie.

Anna says, "Good morning, Danny," and rolls me onto my side, facing the window.

I can't see what she is doing, but from the rustling sounds, followed by the sound of dripping water that I attribute to the ringing out of a sponge, I assume that she is changing and cleaning me. After about nine years of this, it has become only marginally less embarrassing. I prefer it when Cassie is not here for this part.

Anna finishes up and then lifts me into my chair, adjusting my position and placing my head gently against the headrest. My head rolls a little to one side, and she readjusts my headrest to face me forward. I am grateful for this and for the fact that she shares Cassie's view, that I am still cognizant and still me, trapped inside an unresponsive body. This is not a view shared by all, or even most.

"There you go, Danny, let's get you into the day room," she says and wheels me out and into the hallway. I close my eyes until we come to a stop.

"Good morning, Marcus," Anna says as the thin wiry guy strolls into the room wearing sunglasses that are too big for his angular face.

"Morning, can you get me a coffee, it was a late one last night," Marcus says in a flat indifferent tone.

"Burning the candle at both ends?" she says rhetorically.

"Yeah, sure." He walks past her without looking in her direction and slouches down in Cassie's chair. "What's up, Danny boy?"

Anna leaves the room.

Marcus takes off his sunglasses and rubs at his eyes. When he opens them again, they look like the scene of an ice-skating accident, cracked ice with blood frozen into every crack. The dark rings around his eyes make them seem an even brighter blue.

"You don't mind if I take a little nap after Anna fucks off?" he says, raising one eyebrow, "No? Great, thanks, Danny boy."

Anna returns a few minutes later with a cup of coffee and puts it down on the table. "There you go, Marcus, is there anything else I can get for you?"

"No, that's it for now," he replies and puts his sunglasses back on.

"Did you already help Danny with his exercises?" she asks.

"Yeah, of course," he says and pulls one side of his face into a quick dismissive frown.

"Alright, let me know if Danny needs anything," she says and leaves the room.

Marcus stands up and walks around me, out of view, and I hear the television turn on. The room spins, and I am facing the television but slumped to one side in my chair with my face pressed to one side of my headrest.

"There you go, Danny boy," he says and tosses the television remote into my lap. "Just in case you want to change the channel."

He clears his throat behind me and says, "You be a good little bird now and watch TV while I take a power nap."

By the end of the first commercial break, I can hear him snoring a little, and when the screen goes black for a split second, I can see my reflection in the television screen and a slightly smaller copy next to it. We both sit, gape-mouthed and slumped in the same position, one slightly behind the other.

The commercial ends and the man selling exercise equipment comes back on, welcoming me back to the shopping channel, saying that I have only one more hour to take advantage of this special offer.

CHAPTER 8

I am the choreographer

Friday is my favorite day, because Friday is garbage day. Friday is the one day when doors get propped open and left that way, as the cleaning staff that works in the house empties all the trash from various receptacles throughout the house into large, plastic, wheeled bins that are then pushed outside, where they are picked up and emptied later in the day by the garbage truck.

At this time every week, headache or not, I leave my chair and my body and move through the open doors to outside. Everything inside is black and blue with yellow, red, and green fading in from recently handled objects and from people.

Outside, the sky is a much darker blue; the trees, grass, and flowers are yellow, orange, pink, and red, and glow like they are hot. The world is frozen still like a three-dimensional photograph, but I am free to walk around, although I still can't really feel anything, only resistance and rigidity.

People frozen in mid-run leave a yellow vapor trail. The driver and passengers frozen in cars glow, leaving longer yellow lines that expose their route, but the cars themselves are merely dark blue and black silhouettes.

The world has the same color characteristics of thermal imaging that I have seen on a television show, where it was used at night by law enforcement to detect the body heat of drug smugglers at the border.

Although it appears similar, it is not heat that makes things glow in this ossified landscape, but life. If someone touches something, they leave a print for a time like they would with heat, but cars and hot engines do not glow, only people, animals, trees, and flowers glow.

I'm out of the house and off the property, walking toward the nearest town. I see the red figure of a man with an orange dog contrasting the blue-black path. The dog has bright white glowing eyes and its chest fades to greenish-yellow with a purple tinge around it. I keep walking and take a shortcut through a trail in the woods. The whole forest glows brightly, with the spaces between in blue and black.

As I emerge from the forest, everything is black and blue, save for the few glowing people frozen in various actions. Silhouetted rectangular framework is dotted with rows of glowing lights, and as I get closer, I realize that it is a bus. A man stands looking up into the sky with his mouth open allowing the white light to pour from his mouth as well as his eyes that glow from an orange face. There is a black rectangle at the side of his face. I move in closer to study him; the rectangle has a tail that wraps around his ear. I assume that it is a cell phone earpiece like the one I have seen Marcus wear previously.

I am trying to figure out what the man is looking at and move my head next to his, following his gaze to a bright yellow object in the sky. Black power lines obscure my view slightly, and I move closer to the man, to view it from the same angle as him. With my head directly in front of his, I look up and see that there is a bright yellow cross in the sky.

There is a rush of sound, and the cross in the sky becomes a bird, a crow. The bus engine whirrs and rumbles as it pulls away. All the regular color of the world returns, and the world is moving. I look down and I can see my hands and the suit that I am wearing.

I can hear a voice in my head, talking to me, "Are you there?"

I spin around thinking that it is the man that drew my attention to the bird, but he is no longer there.

"Are you still there?" the voice says.

I put my hand up to my head and feel the earpiece attached to my ear and realize that somehow, I am now back in the real world, and I am someone else. Somehow, I have become him, and I attempt to speak.

"Hello?" I say.

"Hey, I thought I'd lost you there," the voice says.

"I'm Daniel," I say.

"What? Where did Jason go?" the voice says.

I am now wondering the same thing. *If I am here in his body, where is he?*

"Who is this?" the voice asks.

My thoughts buzz simultaneously with excitement and panic, and the latter churns my gut.

"Daniel from accounts?" the voice asks.

The world slows to a stop and the colors darken to black and blue, and once again, I am standing next to the man with the earpiece, but he stands in a different position, the position that I left him in.

I leave the scene and make my way back, the same way I came. When I arrive back home, the doors are all still open, and I slip inside. I return back to the day room and to the figure in the wheelchair.

When I left, the body of the figure was dull red in color; now it looks blue-black, the same as the furniture around it, but with a slight green glow in its center. I re-enter my body, and there is pressure and a squeal in my head.

The noise and pain subside over the next short while, and I attempt to make sense of what happened on my walk. I am wondering what the possibilities are, and also what the consequences might be.

CHAPTER 9

I am listening

Cassie has always maintained the view that I am still in here, even after the failure of the last attempt to prove it. She had noticed movement in the index finger of my right hand and had said that she thought that I was trying to communicate. She arranged to have a computer brought in that had software installed that allows the user to scroll through letters with the use of only a single button, which she placed and secured on the arm of my chair, positioned under the finger that was in her opinion, tapping to get her attention.

Cassie explained, both to my parents and to me, how the software worked. Click once for a menu to appear, and then it will scroll through letters. When the letter I wanted to use was on the screen, I should click to select it, and then it would start over. After I got the hang of that, then I would be able to advance to a more efficient system that would evolve with use.

The message I typed was nonsense. The finger movement was something that I was unaware of and not in control of, a twitch, a spasm, a nerve response resulting from some half-chewed control system. This was the last time that my parents got their hopes up and was the last time they visited the day room or me.

***

Cassie says, "They were talking about eye tracking in my course. I thought that maybe we could give it a try. I don't think that your parents are going to approve after the last attempt, but there are relatively inexpensive versions of the equipment. A regular computer and similar software to what we tried before, but there are cameras and sensors that you can plug in and calibrate so that it tracks the movement of your eyes, and you can make selections on screen just by looking at them."

Cassie smiles and touches my hand.

If I can keep control of my eyes for long enough to spell even one word, then they will know that I am still here.

"I'm going to ask my computer guy if there is anything that he can do," she says.

She stares into my eyes and says, "I can't wait to finally speak with you, Danny."

Anna walks into view. "It's almost five, Cass. You are going to be late for your course if you don't get a move on."

"Thanks, Anna, I didn't realize that it was getting so late," Cassie says and begins to gather her things. "Is Marcus here yet?"

"Not yet, but it's okay, I can sit with Danny until he gets here," Anna says.

"Thank you, Anna. I'll leave this here, if you want to read to Danny until Marcus arrives," Cassie says and places the book down on the table.

"I'll do that, Cass, now you'd better get going; don't worry about us. Danny, Frodo, and I will be just fine." Anna smiles and opens the book to the bookmarked page.

***

I hear the Mustang pull into the driveway, and a couple minutes later, Marcus walks into the day room with a girl.

"Hello, Marcus," Anna says, "Who's this?"

"This is Shelly; she wanted to meet Danny boy," he says.

The girl looks down at the floor and shuffles like someone desperate to find a washroom.

"You are not supposed to bring non-staff members into the house," Anna says.

"She's my helper," he says.

"Helper?"

"Don't worry about it; it's fine," Marcus says.

"I don't think that Danny's mother and father would approve of you bringing strangers into their house, no offense, Shelly," Anna says and regards the meek-looking girl as she stands next to Marcus and tugs at his shirt.

"It's okay, I'll go," Shelly says in almost a whisper.

"Are you going to kick her out, Anna?" he says and throws an accusing glance at Anna.

"Well no, but if ... " Anna starts.

"Then there's no problem," Marcus says.

Anna gets up out of the chair and places the bookmark back in the book.

"Alright, I will see you at bedtime, Danny." Anna places the book back on the table and turns to Marcus, "If you have time, maybe you can continue reading to Danny."

Marcus stares at Anna until she leaves the room.

"Who the fuck does she think she is?" he says.

"Maybe I should go," Shelly says.

"Why? Because of *Aunt* Anna?" He raises his eyebrows. "She's a glorified maid, don't worry about it."

He turns to me and says, "What's up, Danny boy?"

"So can he speak or anything?" Shelly says, staring into my eyes the way a kid stares into a fish bowl.

"Nope, just sits there drooling and shitting himself all day," Marcus says.

"That's sad. Can he hear us?" She turns to face him, and the chemical fog of cheap perfume attacks two of my senses.

"No, he's a vegetable," he says.

"Why don't they just put him out of his misery?" she says.

"The laws don't allow it," he says, pulls up another chair, and sets it across the table from his.

Shelly sits down and turns with her arm over the back of the chair to stare at me some more.

"So, what do you do, just sit here?" she asks.

"Pretty much; he's low maintenance. Anna changes him and cleans him," he says.

"Gross," she says scrunching up her face.

"It was a lot more work taking care of old Monty, and I was there all the time. I get paid the same for looking after Danny boy, and I don't have to do anything," he says.

"Except read to him?" she asks.

Marcus picks up the book and takes out the bookmark, replacing it nearer the back. "I'm not reading that dungeons and dragons shit."

"Marcus," Shelly exclaims.

"What? He can't understand it anyway," he says and places the book back down on the table. He extends his arm and puts a hand on Shelly's leg, "You want to … "

"No, not in front of him," she says, cutting him off.

"Why not? He is brain dead, what does he care?"

"He's looking right at us," she says.

Marcus stands up, takes off his coat, throws it toward me, and everything goes black. "Night-night, little bird, go to sleep."

"Marcus?" she says in a tone that seems to contrast her mousy demeanor.

After a couple minutes of muffled reluctance, reasoning and giggling, I hear him grunting and her stifling intermittent moans.

CHAPTER 10

I am still here

There are extension cords and cables leading to the table and a computer screen sitting on it. Cassie is sitting in her chair. Her face is tinted blue, lit by the screen, and her eyes flick from one direction to another.

"Sorry this is taking so long, Danny, I want to make sure that it's properly calibrated before we get started," Cassie says.

My headache is near unbearable right now. I want to leave my body, to take a break from the pain, but I stay and wait. After today, I will be able to ask for painkillers to deal with my headaches, and I will finally be able to talk to her. I will be able to ask her to go back and read the chapters that Marcus skipped. I will be able to thank Cassie and Aunt Anna for everything that they have done. I will be able to talk, to communicate, to rejoin the living, and help them understand what it is like to be trapped in here.

Anna walks in. "Looks like something described in one of your science fiction novels."

"It's pretty simple; all the letters are on the right-hand side, and you choose a letter by looking at it, then other boxes open up and expand as you look toward them. It predicts the next letter to follow your previous selection based on probability and shows those letters in the bigger boxes," Cassie says.

"Sounds complicated," Anna says.

"The more you use it, the quicker it gets. It learns what words you use regularly and in conjunction with others, and then multiple options pop up in boxes after you start a word, like predictive text on your phone," Cassie says.

Anna's expression doesn't change. "It takes me twenty minutes to send a text on my phone."

I am practicing moving my eyes. They are not doing exactly what I want, and every time I strain to look left, the pain in my head rings out like a church bell.

Marcus enters the room and says, "What's going on?"

"Cassie thinks that Danny might be able to communicate to us, using his eyes," Anna says, moving her eyes around as she explains which makes me laugh inside.

"It's the Dasher software, modified for eye tracking control," Cassie adds.

"Didn't you already try something like this?" Marcus says with a sour look on his face.

"It's different software, and that was with a push switch for his finger," Cassie says.

"What's the difference?" Marcus asks.

"The finger movement turned out to be involuntary, but it doesn't mean that Danny's not in there. They use something similar to this for sufferers of locked-in syndrome who can only move their eyes up and down," Cassie says.

"So what if it doesn't work?" Marcus says.

Cassie turns and stares at Marcus. "I don't know, Marcus. I guess we just make him as comfortable as possible and go back to the way we were before, *hoping* that he's still in there and *treating* him like he is."

I am reminded of various stories from Cassie's childhood, of her chastising her foster brother, Brian. From the sharpness in Cassie's tone, I wonder if she is aware of how Marcus behaves toward me, when she is not here.

"Don't you have a course to go to?" Marcus says with enough bite in his tone to satisfy his need for retaliation.

"I just want to get this set up first," Cassie says.

Cassie turns the screen carefully, and then pushes my chair in as close to the table as it will go. The screen is bright and hurts my eyes. The light makes my headache worse, and as I blink, I can see colored boxes opening and growing bigger on the screen.

"It's going to take a little practice, Danny," Cassie says and then turns to Marcus, "You don't have to do anything, just leave Danny in front of the screen and give him a chance to get used to the interface. Anna will come and check on him later and take him to bed."

"I will make sure that everything is okay here, Cass," Anna says.

"I really wanted to be here for this," Cassie says.

Marcus peers around the screen and watches as the colored boxes expand.

"Don't put your head in the way, Marcus, just sit out of the way and give Danny a chance to figure it out," Cassie says, and turns to me, "I'm going to try to get back before you go to bed, Danny."

Anna and Cassie walk away together, and I lose them in the darkness beyond the bright screen. I have to shut my eyes for a couple minutes to let my headache settle.

Marcus peers around the screen again and reads aloud the text in the box at the top of the screen, "Acabyzyyaa." He turns to me. "Wow, is that Shakespeare." He sits back down in Cassie's chair, shaking his head.

I look back at the screen and colored boxes begin to scroll and expand from the right-hand side. The letters are from A to Z, top to bottom, down the right-hand side, and as I look at one of the letters, it grows and moves to the left, then other boxes grow larger from the right-hand side, and random letters move quickly from right to left, stacking up to produce yet another nonsensical sentence. I stare at an empty box and the sentence is removed.

I look again at the letters on the right-hand side and at the H, then move my eyes away to the left, back to the e, then away, then l, l, o, _, m, y, _, n, a, m, e, _, i, s, _, D, a, n, i, e, l.

I continue to write, "It has been so long since I have had a chance to say anything. I don't know what to write. I am very thankful that you have never given up hope that I can hear you. Cassie, you are my angel. Without you, I would not have wanted to go on living. When you are here, I no longer feel trapped, and when you read to me, it allows me to escape, no longer bound by this chair; I am free, following Frodo on his quest or following a postman across an apocalyptic landscape. I look forward to wonderful conversations with you. I do have a request, and it is for pain medication to help with my headaches. They come and go, but are sometimes so painful that I cannot see or hear. Cassie, this is the greatest gift anyone has ever given to me, the ability to rejoin the world as a real person. Oh, and by the way, in my opinion Cassie, that boy did not deserve you in the first place. You need a nice guy with a sense of humor. Knock. Knock."

Marcus stands up and moves around me. "What the fuck?"

I can hear him breathing over my shoulder as he reads the text on the screen, "Knock, knock?"

Anna says from somewhere, "What was that? Did he write something?"

"What? No. It just looks like random letters. Can you get me a glass of water, please?" Marcus says.

"*Please?*" Anna says in surprise, "I think that is the first time you have ever said *please*."

"I just don't want to miss it if Danny boy starts to write," he says.

After Anna leaves the room, Marcus turns the screen and leans toward it for a few seconds, his eyes flicking to the right and up and down.

"If you can talk, you'll get me fired. There's no way I'll get another job if all the shit you've seen goes on my file. Sorry, little bird, but you're not going to say a word," Marcus says, then unplugs something from the back of the computer and turns the screen back to me.

The message at the top is now a stream of vowels, and the boxes no longer expand when I look at the letters to the right.

Anna walks back in and hands the glass to Marcus, "Anything yet?"

"I don't think so, take a look," Marcus says and takes a drink.

Anna leans her head around the screen for a second and I hear the air pour out of her. "Cassie really thought this would work," Anna says and looks down at the floor.

"If Danny *is* in there, then he knows that we will do *whatever* we have to," he says.

Anna says, "I'll be back later to take Danny to bed."

"Ok, thanks, Anna," Marcus says, imitating a smile.

On the outside, I am calm and still. Inside, I am screaming, I am shouting, I am begging, and crying. *Please, please. Plug it back in. Let me speak. I won't tell anyone about you, Marcus. Please. Don't lock me back in here. Please.*

CHAPTER 11

I am the open wound

I follow closely behind. The hunt has been long and grueling, lasting almost three days. My jeans are soaked to above the knee, and the sleeves of my hooded sweater are also wet. The ground is soft and spongy under foot, and he shoots me a glance every time a twig snaps under my boots. He walks carefully and silently with bare feet, wearing only a loincloth that is the same earthy color as his skin. He carries a small tubular wicker basket that hangs at his waist from a string over one shoulder and a long bamboo tube wrapped with old cloth and leather strips.

He turns, and from a crouched position, he spreads his fingers in my direction, and I stop and wait. I worry that I will scare off whatever it is that he has seen or heard and make every effort to stay silent. I can hear myself swallow, and I have an urge to cough, a tickle in my throat that I am trying desperately to ignore. He slowly reaches into the wicker basket and withdraws a dart. He spins the dart between the palms of his hands to fluff up the material to obtain a better air seal in the blowgun, and then he dips the tip into a small section of bamboo that is sealed at one end and lashed to the inside of the wicker basket. He feeds the dart into the blowgun and raises it vertically to his lips before lowering the end to aim and puffing out his cheeks. I follow the blowgun to what he is aiming at, and he forcefully exhales the projectile.

For a couple seconds, I think that he has missed, then the animal goes limp and crashes down through small tree limbs, getting hung up on a limb around halfway down. He gestures for me to take the blowgun and then climbs the tree with the agility and ease that I would associate with the animal he is going to collect. He frees the animal and tosses it to the ground, where it lands with a wet thud, next to me. The small monkey that he has killed will go toward feeding the people of his village, and by this point, I am somewhat desensitized to the killing of animals. To him and his family, the animals of the forest are food; it is how they survive. It is my task to carry the dead animal back to the village, along with whatever quarry has been caught or killed in the traps that were set.

***

For three days, I have been stalking through the Amazon, or at least a memory of the Amazon. The singular goal of the native that I follow is to kill and procure food. The singular thing that I will kill on the hunt is time.

Cassie has not read to me for three days. The day that I attempted to write a letter to her, I heard her crying in the hallway outside my room. Cassie was sitting in the chair when Anna wheeled me into the day room the next day and cried again when she looked into my eyes. Seeing her cry, seeing her heart broken, hurts more than knowing that I will never again have the chance to speak with her. Knowing that Marcus did this to me is not what fills me with the now constant burning hatred. It is what Marcus has done to Cassie that has done this. My world has become an open wound, and Marcus Salt has poured in.

The target of my anger seems to switch back and forth from the cold-blooded reptile named Marcus, to the useless gape-mouth sculpture that I haunt, and even to the long dead parasite that destroyed so much of my brain. The parasite led my own immune system into beginning a never-ending war against the scar tissue left by each cyst, which would eventually do more damage than the tapeworm itself.

Cassie says, "I have a training day tomorrow."

"Are you okay, Cass?" Anna asks.

"No, not really," Cassie says.

"We can't give up hope; he might still be in there, Cassie," Anna says.

"I know." Cassie looks up at Anna. "That's the part that upsets me. If Danny *is* in there and he can't ever communicate, then what kind of life is that? What if he's trapped in there, screaming at me all day, every day, to unplug everything and put him out of his misery? What if he hates the books that I read to him? What if everything that I have done to try and make Danny's life just a little better has been torture for him?"

"Cass?" Anna says and puts a hand on Cassie's shoulder.

"I haven't felt like this since Emily passed away," Cassie says and begins to sob again.

Anna cradles Cassie's head. "She would be proud of everything you have done for Danny and who you have become.

CHAPTER 12

I am rotting meat

My grandfather, Montgomery Stockholm, was generally a well-respected and well-liked man. I loved my grandfather, and I miss him. I did not attend his funeral and was unaware of his passing until months after the event.

Some of my fondest memories as a child were of fishing trips with my grandfather. He would tell me stories from his childhood while we sat in a two-man rowboat holding rods and hardly ever catching any fish. When we did catch a fish, he would skin and debone it right away before packing the meat in salt. He told me that this was the way that meat had been preserved for centuries and that sometimes salt is also used to hide the taste of spoiling meat. He grew up poor, and his parents did not have a refrigerator, so they would pack their meat in salt.

Most of the stories he told me included petty crime, stealing bread from the bakery or fish from the fishmongers. When I listened to his stories, I would always picture it in my mind like the 1948 *Oliver Twist* movie, but I never let on that fact to my grandfather. He made his money later on in life as a realtor and grew his wealth with a few lucky investments in companies that grew almost overnight, which made him a multi-millionaire. He hardly ever discussed his wealth and seemed to derive more joy in talking to me about the years in which he was young and poor.

My grandfather would come over for dinner every Friday evening, when my parents and I were not off in some remote part of the world. Sometimes, the dinner would become a dinner party with other guests, and my grandfather would hide out in the day room, which at that time was a study.

Whenever I noticed him missing, I would make my way to the day room, and he would replace his smoking pipe with a finger to his lips and wink. He made no secret of not liking the formality of the dinner parties and had said to me on occasion that he couldn't understand why a whole room full of people half his age acted more like old farts than friends his own age.

After I was paralyzed, my grandfather spent a lot more time in the dayroom and would continue to tell me stories from when he was a young man. He no longer smoked his pipe in there but sat in the same leather chair. Even in my condition, I think my grandfather felt that he still had more in common with me, than with the high-class entourage that had attached itself to my family.

My eighteenth birthday would be the last I would spend with my grandfather. He sat and talked to me about all of my past birthdays and about some of his. I assume that everyone had left it to someone else to inform me of my grandfather's illness; maybe the staff believed that the news should be, or had been, delivered by a family member, and maybe my parents had believed the opposite.

Over a year later, Marcus arrived in the day room and informed Cassie that he would be helping her perform her duties and would be relief care for me now that Monty was gone. He also said that this had been something that my grandfather had explicitly asked of him, before he died. This is how I learned of my grandfather's passing—a flippant remark from the palliative care helper, Marcus Salt. I didn't like Marcus from his first sentence, and over time, I wondered how he had managed to fool my grandfather into asking him to stay.

Salt is rarely used anymore to preserve meat, but is still often used to hide the taste of rotting meat.

CHAPTER 13

I am the remote controller

I hear the Mustang pull into the driveway. The engine shuts off and I hear the door shut. I hear Anna greet Marcus in the foyer. I see him enter the room in my periphery, and I watch the shape of him come into my field of vision. He is wearing sunglasses, and I want him to take them off and look me in the eyes. He keeps them on and sits down in Cassie's chair. He doesn't greet me the way he usually does, and after ten minutes of my eyes burning holes into his flesh, he turns my chair and turns on the television.

I watch the green lines stack on the screen as he turns the volume up, way louder than it needs to be, and I wonder if this is an attempt to drown out the sound of his conscience.

Between special offers on the shopping channel, I hear Marcus talking to Anna.

"You look like you're taking this as hard as the rest of us," Anna says.

It cuts vegetables.

"Yeah, it's hard to look at him, knowing that he's not really in there," Marcus says.

It cuts meat.

"We don't know that; he might still be in there. Cassie is right, we shouldn't just give up," Anna says.

It slices meat.

"Maybe no one will ever know if he's in there or not," Marcus says.

Call now, or you'll miss this special offer.

"Don't be so pessimistic, Marcus. Who knows what will happen in the future with technology and medicine?" Anna says.

This is your last chance to take advantage of this one-time deal.

The blue light from the television spreads around the room as I stand up and walk toward the hallway, passing Anna and Marcus. I make my way through the house and into the kitchen, where I see a glowing yellow figure that I assume is the cook. I move toward him and the world unfreezes as the color returns. It takes a second to shake off the vertigo-like sensation before I snatch up a knife from the block, and with my head down and purpose in my heavy steps, I storm back toward the dayroom.

I turn the corner, and as I glance up, I see the cook clutching the knife. He is small in the mirror at the end of the hallway, and I stop at the day room entrance, staring at his reflection in the mirror.

An image from memory flashes in my mind. I'm looking down the length of a blowgun at a beautiful multicolored bird. I'm thinking that this is no longer a bird, but food for the families of the village. This is how they live. This is how they survive.

I take a breath and let the air fill my cheeks. I steady my aim. I hesitate, with my breath held for too long, and begin to shake. I try to silence the conflict in my conscience, but I cannot, and I cannot kill the bird. This is *not* how I have lived or how I have survived. I hand the blowgun quietly to the hunter at my side, and without hesitation, he exhales the dart through the bird's chest. It flutters for a second and falls still to the wet ground below.

***

As I stare at the cook, I know that I cannot do it, but not for the same reason I couldn't kill the bird. Whether I can bring myself to kill or not, I can't let an innocent man be condemned to a cage for the rest of his life for my actions. I let go of the knife.

Anna looks over at me before the world turns blue and turns to stone. I walk over, stop an inch away from Marcus, and glare into the white lights where his eyes should be. *You are a lucky little bird.*

I return to my chair and sit down. The world resumes speed, and I hear the knife hit the floor, followed by a thud and slap.

Beyond the squealing and stabbing pain, I hear Anna say, "Oh my God are you okay?"

"What happened?" Marcus asks.

"I don't know; he was just standing in the doorway and then he collapsed," Anna says. "Help me turn him."

"What's wrong with him?" Marcus says.

"Call an ambulance," Anna says.

I listen as Marcus gives the details over the phone.

"I don't know; he just collapsed. I think he hit his head when he hit the floor," Marcus says.

"No. I don't think so. He's the cook. I don't know. Okay," Marcus says intermittently.

He gives the address, and we wait as the dance soundtrack of the workout DVD infomercial plays.

You can really feel it in the pit of your stomach.

This will change your life.

I can hear the siren in the distance.

This will help you drop that unwanted weight.

The siren grows louder, and I can see the lights reflecting off the walls in the dayroom and off of the television screen.

Now we're going to drop to the floor and relax for a minute.

Anna leads the paramedics in, and I hear them trying to talk to the cook, asking if he can hear them.

You can really feel the burn.

One, two, three, and lift.

I hear the paramedics ready the stretcher, "Three, two, one, lift."

A minute later, the ambulance pulls out, and the siren fades out behind the sound of the television, telling me of the *one-time-only, life-changing opportunity* that I have now missed.

CHAPTER 14

I am animal

Cassie says, "I'm so sorry, Danny. I'm sorry that I have been quiet and withdrawn, and I'm sorry if you don't like the books that I read to you, or if you are sick of hearing about my life. I'm sorry if you are sick of my problems when they pale in comparison to what I can only imagine you endure every day. I'm sorry that I don't hear you or know what you want, and I'm sorry if anything I do or say makes it worse. I'm sorry if I got your hopes up, like I did my own."

If Cassie had never spoken to me again, I would have understood. Without her, I would have nothing to want to live for, not that will or want in any way affect my standard of living, but I can see what this last failed attempt to communicate has done to her, and it breaks my heart.

***

Over the course of almost nine years that she has cared for me, I have learned a great deal about her life and the events that have helped to shape her into the strong and beautiful person she is. I know her better than anyone else does. I know that her parents were both drunks and that she was taken away by social services after a fight between her parents spilled out onto the front lawn. The fight landed her dad with an assault charge, and as the police were putting him in handcuffs, her mom jumped on the back of the arresting officer and bit his ear, which earned *her* an assault charge also.

Cassie was taken into foster care, and from the stories that she has told me, most of the families that took her in, it would seem, did so only for the government check. She was not abused, or beaten, or any of the foul things that you hear horror stories about from foster care. At best, she was treated with mild neglect and indifference, and at worst, made to feel like a burden. She grew up with many different siblings. Brian was the foster brother that she had for the longest time; although, they were never really that close. She has maintained casual contact with him over the years via sporadic phone conversations, but they rarely ever see each other.

She was moved around from home to home for whatever reason, and was eventually taken in by Emily Mathews, namesake of the Emily Mathews foundation for under-privileged children, which coincidentally, was one of the charities that regularly received generous donations from my mother and father and probably still does.

Emily's husband had passed away unexpectedly when she was in her thirties. She had refused to ever replace the love of her life but had always wanted children and so she began fostering. She became known for her kindness and her many years raising happy children that would all congregate back at her house for every holiday or family get-together, bringing with them their children, and eventually, grandchildren. Cassie was the last child to be fostered and was later adopted by Emily.

Emily had given her all the love and security that a child could ask for and allowed her the opportunity of a good home and good schooling. Cassie was a good student, particularly enjoyed biology and chemistry, and hoped for a career in medical science. After seeing her mother grow old and require constant care, Cassie had altered the course of her education to better suit a career in nursing. She had taken care of Emily until her last breath. Cassie continued in her efforts to become a nurse and volunteered at the nursing home where my Aunt Anna worked, and they would later employ Cassie full-time.

Years later, she and Anna left the nursing home to perform live-in care for me, and have done ever since.

CHAPTER 15

I am vegetable

A large percentage of the doctors and specialists that have seen and studied me over the past nine years are of the opinion that I am no longer the Danny that my parents knew. At first, they would talk about me in hushed voices or behind hospital doors, and I would just watch their mouths move. My father would become visibly agitated, and my mother would begin to cry, shooting glances back at me through the glass.

After a couple years, they would no longer leave the room or talk out of earshot. The doctors would deliver news of my condition in a very matter-of-fact way, the way a car mechanic delivers news of a blown head-gasket. They would talk about the chance of me being cognizant or in a vegetative state, but in their opinion, more likely the latter. After various scans, they would inform my parents of how much of my brain had been eaten away, and that there was no way of stopping my body from attacking the scar tissue and destroying even more of my brain. On occasion, I was positioned in such a way that I could see the scanned images, resembling cauliflower with the perforated characteristic of Swiss cheese.

I have gotten used to people staring into the bowl from inches away, tapping on the glass to see if I will respond, and I remain hidden in the eye socket of an inanimate skull, waiting for the intruding voyeur to leave.

Over time, my parents relented to the idea that I was gone. I think that this was the only way for them to cope with the loss of their son; if I was gone, then they could mourn and grieve, and eventually, move on. I would still catch the odd glimmer of hope in my mother as various options to try to communicate with me were exhausted, the last of which, was the twitching finger.

I had overheard my mother ask doctors and specialists for help, and occasionally, she had asked God for help, but none were seemingly able. I have done a great deal of pleading with God, but after nine years straining to hear the faintest murmur, I have given up on the idea of a god, or at least the idea of a god that cares about me.

CHAPTER 16

I am mineral

I look like a one-hundred-and-sixty-pound lump of clay, a face punched into it and adorned with asymmetric features, eyes in the sunken knuckle indents, a nose formed by the gap between my creator's middle fingers, and a gaping hole spooned out of the clay for a mouth.

If we were all created in God's image, then maybe I am just a poor representation, a degrading sculpture produced by incompetent or inexperienced hands and an embarrassment to God. Maybe I am a perfect re-creation of God, and this is why he, like me, is no longer able to communicate and why countless daily prayers go unanswered. Maybe life is a test, and maybe I failed that test before reaching adulthood. Maybe that is why I have been locked in purgatory for the last nine years, or maybe there is no God, no heaven, and no hell.

***

To Marcus, I am a one-hundred-and-sixty-pound lump of gold, which he will harvest, nugget by nugget, to pay for the upkeep of a bright red 1972 Mustang, a new car stereo that almost drowns out the sound of the engine, and designer sunglasses that hide the effects of an over-active social life. He will use the harvested mineral to pay for the rented luxury penthouse apartment that he boasts about frequently on his brand new top-of-the-line cell phone, which allows me insight to his life vicariously through eavesdropped conversations with what he would call his friends.

"I'm here for a couple hours; I'll swing by after," Marcus says into the phone.

"Oh yeah? No, I'm done with that one, she's too needy." He leans on the table and peers out of the window, presumably to admire his prize possession, the 1972 Mustang.

"How old are they?" He pulls out his keys and points them at the glass. I hear a *peep* and there is a brief yellow flash.

"So I guess I'm buying the booze." He sits back down in Cassie's chair and leans back, running a hand through hair that is unaffected by the gesture.

"Cassie gets here at eight," he says.

"Danny boy's nurse." He looks me in the eyes for the first time in over a week.

"She's alright, I'd fuck it," he says through a smirk, and winks at me.

"Alright, later." He sets his phone down gently on the table.

"I feel bad for you, Danny boy, there's a lot of pussy in this world that you are missing out on, guess that just leaves more for me though," he says and raises his eyebrows.

Marcus leans forward on the table between us. "Even if you *could* talk, who would be interested in anything you have to say?"

"Knock, knock." He punctuates the words with the rap of his knuckles on the table.

"Who's there?" he says and shakes his head slowly, "No one."

CHAPTER 17

I am the author

"They told him it was a grand mal seizure," Anna says.

"Did they say what caused it?" Cassie holds my arm outstretched and pauses for a beat to look at Anna.

"No, but he says that he has to go back for more tests; he says that he was in the kitchen preparing food for the next day and then he doesn't remember anything, until he woke up in the hospital," Anna says.

"Is he going to be okay?" Cassie continues to contract my arm at the elbow, steps around to my right, and begins to rotate my shoulder.

"He seems fine now; he said they want to test him for epilepsy," Anna says.

Cassie pulls her chair in close and sits down. Her lips are tight together and her brow furrowed. As she rolls my wrist in her hands, she says, "Poor guy."

She interlocks her fingers with mine. "Today is the last day of my course. Did you call Marcus?"

Anna moves behind Cassie and stares through the window. "I left a message for him yesterday to be here in the morning. I guess I should have been more specific." The morning sun falls into the long lines grooved into her cheek that now appear the same color as the dark pink where her lips meet.

"I can probably still call them and ask to go in the evening instead," Cassie says with my other hand now in hers.

One of my eyes decides to rest, and the other struggles to focus. I let them close, and I can no longer *feel* Cassie's touch.

"Don't worry about it, Cass, I'll take care of Danny," Anna says.

"I started reading *The Chrysalids* to Danny; I can leave it here, if you want to read to him." I hear the dampened jingling of keys and open my eyes as Cassie pulls the book from her bag and places it on the table.

"I'll do that, Cass. I'm sure his highness, Marcus, will show up at some point." As Anna turns away from the sun, the pink lines blend into the blue-black shadows of her skin.

Cassie stands up and puts her arms around Anna. "I'm so glad he has you, Anna."

The shape of Anna's arms seems cut out of the back of Cassie's white uniform. "You're a good woman, Cass, we are all lucky to have you in our lives."

"Thank you, Anna." Cassie lets go of Anna and gathers her things. "I had better go."

Cassie turns back to me. "I'll be back after my course Danny."

Anna says, "I'll see you later, Cass."

"See you later." Cassie smiles and walks out of my view.

Anna sits down across the table and smiles at me as if recalling a happy memory of the boy she once knew. She begins to read from the bookmarked page, and I let the words play like a movie in my head.

***

Anna's voice is eventually drowned out by the sound of the Mustang's engine, accompanied by a thumping bass metronome. A few minutes later, Marcus saunters into the dayroom.

Anna places the book down on the table and turns to Marcus. "Good *morning*, Marcus."

"Morning," he says.

There is an awkward moment between them before Anna relinquishes the chair to Marcus and asks him if he would like coffee.

He nods and sits down opposite me as Anna exits the room.

Marcus picks up the book and moves the bookmark forward about forty or so pages, which bothers me more than it usually does. I make extra effort and move my gaze between lolls, back and forth from him, to the book.

He studies me for a minute and frowns. "What? You want me to read some more to you?" he says and picks up the book.

"Once upon a time, there was a shit book that I'm not going to read to you. The end," he says and places the bookmark at the back before closing the book.

He removes his sunglasses and sets them over my eyes. "It's rude to stare."

Anna returns a few minutes later with his coffee, and looking at me, she says, "What's going on here Marcus?"

"What?" he says.

"Why is Danny wearing your sunglasses?" she asks.

Marcus rolls his eyes and yawns.

"Here, looks like you *need* this," Anna says and puts the cup down firmly on the table.

"What the hell is this?" Anna picks up the book and pulls the bookmark from the back. "There's no way you read all of that while I was making your coffee. If you don't want to read to Danny then don't, but leave the bookmark where it is."

Marcus stares up at Anna for a second. "Why don't you run off and mind your own business, and let me do my job."

"Excuse me?" Anna says, "It *is* my business. Why don't you actually *do* your job, instead of just sitting there?"

"Who the fuck do you think you are?" he says and glares at her.

"I have been a part of this family since long before Danny was even born. Danny is my nephew; who do you think *you* are? I don't know how you still have a job. You are nothing but a disrespectful child and a leech on this family," Anna says and walks out of view.

I watch his eyes follow her out, and under his breath, he says, "Fucking nigger."

I leave my body and exit the room. I move around the large glowing figure of Anna in the hallway and continue out through the open doors at the back of the house.

There is a glowing orange figure pouring blue trash into one of the garbage containers outside, and I make my way toward him. Without breaking step, I collide with the figure and the pungent smell of garbage fills my nose, his nose. Blue and yellow fade quickly to the greys and greens of the real world and sound begins abruptly. I drop the empty garbage can and steady myself, holding on to the side of the large green bin. I make my way around to the front of the house, checking the man's pockets and retrieving the staff keys to the house.

I see the bright red 1972 Mustang parked on the blacktop driveway in front of the house, and I hike across the grass and gravel toward it with the keys clenched in my fist. I make sure that Marcus is not watching through the dayroom window, just feet away, and stoop down next to the driver side door, digging the key into the paint and carving with deep straight lines.

On my way back to the garbage can, I pick the red paint from the grooves of the key and return them to the same pocket. I pick up the garbage can and hold it out in roughly the same position it was in, before leaving the body and returning to my own.

CHAPTER 18

I am ready

"Who the fuck did it?" Marcus stands with his bony fists balled up and his face sticking out about ten inches in front of the rest of him.

"How should I know? I've been in here the whole time; why don't you ask the cleaners?" Anna says.

"I'm going to find out who did it, *Anna*," he says.

"Maybe someone just walked by and scraped it by accident," Anna says, shrugging her shoulders.

"It says, 'Knock, knock,'" Marcus shouts.

"Hey, don't yell at me, I didn't do it," Anna snaps.

"No? Well, whoever did is paying for a new paint job. That's the original paint," he says.

Anna turns and leaves the room, shaking her head, and Marcus stares at me. "I know she fucking saw that note. You can say goodbye to *Aunt* Anna; I'm going to have that cunt arrested."

His phone vibrates on the table. He looks at it and ignores it. When it stops vibrating, it says missed call, and I notice that the time is 5:46. Cassie won't be here until around 8:00 this evening.

I watch him tapping on the table and cursing under his breath.

"What the fuck are you looking at?" he says, glaring into my eyes.

I would love to have the use of my body for long enough to deny him the further use of his.

Marcus stands up and spins my chair around to face the television. My body slumps sideways, then forward, and the floor accelerates to meet my face. I hear a *pop* and *hiss*, and see one of the apparatus stands fall slowly to the ground. Inside, I flinch as it lands inches from my outwardly unresponsive face.

"Fuck," Marcus shouts, and I see him reach down to pick up the stand.

My vision starts to blur and does so increasingly with a distorted pulsing rhythm as colors begin to appear like electrical sparks in front of my eyes. My field of vision begins to narrow, and there is immense pressure inside my head. I begin to panic as my senses are replaced with kaleidoscopic color and a high-pitched squealing. Everything is swallowed by darkness, and a dull throbbing pulse beats in my head.

The pulsing lights begin to slow, and shapes move in front of me. A low rhythmic murmur of mechanical sound swells; from somewhere, there comes alternating sounds, like a blowtorch gasping for breath between bursts of flame. The smell of bodily excretion is strong in my nostrils, and the sounds evolve into the *whir* and *hiss* of medical apparatus. Greasy representations of light move from right to left, and a black cross settles in the center of my view. A black shape moves in front of the light and descends to one side of the cross.

I can hear what I think is Anna's voice. It sounds dull, and every syllable that rises in tone is accompanied by a tinny ringing whine. I cannot understand what she is saying. The light is obscured by another black blur, and more muffled voices utter dull vowel sounds that I cannot understand. A sudden pain stabs its way through the side of my head, and all I can hear is squealing. The sound seems wrapped around whatever is drilling through my head, and sharp electrical shocks travel the wiring of my brain.

The sharp pain begins to dissipate and is replaced with a dull but lingering pain. The oscillating squeal serves as background music to a singular thought. *I hope that this is what it feels like to die.*

CHAPTER 19

I am an epidemic

The windows of my cage are smeared with grease, and I can no longer see through them. I can only make out fragments of conversation between the distorted blaring high-pitched tones, like that of a nursery rhyme played through the speakers of an ice cream truck.

Cassie's voice hurts like brain freeze. Tinny crackled consonants and screeching siren vowels cut through the white noise, and I strain to understand any of it. From the odd word spoken in a lower register or maybe lower volume, and with me having to fill in the gaps between, I think that she is saying something about someone being tested for meningitis or encephalitis.

Anna asks something, and I can tell it is a question because of the rising intonation, but I can't make out the words.

Marcus speaks, and through the hiss, I can make out *his* every word. "I have to get checked out?"

Cassie whistles and drags her nails down a chalkboard.

The only thing that I catch from Anna's response is "Grand mal seizures."

I hear Cassie's heels on the floor, moving away, and each step echoes with a squeal. The shrill exchange continues, and my heart begins to sink, knowing that I will never hear her soft voice again.

Marcus hisses, "So everyone has to get checked out? Mr. and Mrs. Stockholm, the cleaners?"

Anna adds dissonant harmony to the screeching chorus.

"I'm not calling Shelly about some bogus epidemic," Marcus hisses.

Cassie's voice carves through the static and the note rings out as I leave my chair. I view the three yellow glowing figures in the room and push my eyes to meet the white glow of his. Color returns as does *my* vision and I am standing opposite Cassie. I glance back at the chair, and for the first time, I feel sympathy for the creature in it.

Cassie says, "Marcus, two people have collapsed after suffering grand mal seizures; it's unlikely that it is just a coincidence."

I walk slowly toward Anna, and she gives me a puzzled look. "Goodbye, Anna," I say and put my arms around her.

Anna flinches for a second and says, "What are you doing? Where are you going?"

I let go of her and approach Cassie who is wearing the same expression as Anna. I put my arms around her and hold her gently.

"What are you doing, Marcus?" Cassie says.

"Goodbye, Cassie," I say.

I want to tell her that I love her, but I know that it is his face that she sees and his voice that she hears. I pull away and walk back toward my chair.

"Goodbye, Danny," I say as I pick up the machine stand and pull it, sparking as it pries free from the wall socket and away from Danny.

There is a pop and hiss as the air expels from the reserve. In a continuous motion, I turn and lift, hurling the machine through the dayroom window. The glass clangs and shatters all over the table, all over me, and then the floor. I stand for a couple seconds admiring the bright red 1972 Mustang parked right outside the window that now has my ventilator half-embedded in the spider-webbed windshield and resting in a dent caved into the black stripe on the hood.

I turn back to Danny, "You're free, little bird."

The world freezes as I pull away from Marcus, and I stand for a while enjoying the silence, trying to work up the courage to experience the pain of my own death and to brave what may come after.

I return to Danny, and I am pulled toward him. The freight train screeches its wheels on the tracks but doesn't stop. The commotion of panicked screaming and clipping heels gunning up and down the dayroom and hallway begins to equalize with the squeal in my own head. Everything is screaming, shouting, then the sound folds in on itself, and the pain in my head is gone. The color pulsing in and out behind my eyelids goes from green to red and slows to a complete stop.

There are two glowing figures frozen in a blur of erratic yellow vapor. One appears to be leaning over the sprawled out yellow-green shape of Marcus on the floor. Small shards of the same color are scattered about his body and fade out into blue. I move toward Cassie and the now dimly lit figure in the chair and I close in to re-enter my body and make the transition to wherever it is that we go. I push my face close and touch the shoulders of the sitting figure, but the world is still frozen. The cage door is once again locked but with me now on the outside. I am trapped in limbo between this world and the next. I am suddenly afraid but have no stomach to churn, no heart to beat faster, and no pulse to race.

I use Marcus as a step up to the chair and then climb up on the table and through the jagged frame of the glassless window, dropping to the black shape of a 1972 Mustang and then to the ground.

II

CHAPTER 20

I am his wasted life

I have been out of my body for what would be days, weeks, maybe even months, going over events of my life, trying to determine the exact cause for my continued punishment. I have gotten used to the colors and the fact that the world will be frozen forever. I could not interact with the moving world around me while trapped inside my frozen body, and I cannot interact with the frozen world as I move around it now. It appears that I have only been moved from the confines of my cage to a much larger, darker prison.

***

I walk across the uneven surface of a solid ocean. The various life forms glow beneath the tinted glass like green stars. I continue to walk toward groups of lights and vague dark angular shapes. As I get closer, I realize that it is the harbor. Rows of shapes embedded in the frozen ocean become boats. Glowing spots become the still and brightly colored afterthoughts of people. Scattered sporadically are stone statues of men or women in mid-stride of a walk or run, some of which seem to defy gravity. A bright glowing couple sit locked in an eternal embrace, and my thoughts return to Cassie.

I keep moving along straight dark lines, a path lit with figures and fenced in by stripes of light. I follow the trails of light that wind into the distance between the orange glow of field and forest and the odd light comes into view in the distance, an animal or bird. I keep on walking.

The trail of light ends with seated figures, and I can just make out the dark outlines of the cars that encapsulate them. I cross through the colored vapor that the traffic has left perpendicular to the trail I followed and see the dotted lights and figures that fill the streets further down.

There is a group of people circling something, and I move in closer to see a dimly lit figure lying on the ground between them. I pass between two of the onlookers to view the figure on the ground. There is a dull light that emits from the center of the figure and a bright light that hovers three feet above. As I stare at the figure on the ground, I begin to feel heavy, and as if pulled by some unseen magnetic force, I am drawn down toward the figure. There is a brief flash of light before everything is immediately enveloped by blackness.

CHAPTER 21

I am awake

There is a bright light in front of my eye and pressure around it. The light moves away to reveal a figure as it recedes back into the blurred white room. I see dark shapes coming toward my other eye and flinch, turning my head away. I can hear the familiar rhythmic beep of hospital equipment and groaning.

"I think he's awake. Go get Dr. Galloway," a voice says.

I try to ask what is happening but what comes out is a slurred mess of vowels and throat sounds.

A black line appears in front of my face. "I need you to try and follow my finger."

The finger blurs out of focus and everything turns black and red.

***

There are people talking and I try to open my eyes.

"There hasn't been any further activity since yesterday?"

"Nothing yet, Doctor."

"Has he been tested for pupil dilation?"

"Not since yesterday. He's just been changed, and I'm about to switch out the IV bag."

I try to call out and hear someone groan.

"I think he's waking up again, Doctor."

"Can you hear me?"

I open my eyes and turn my head away from the light. There is a figure dressed in blue that blurs in and out of focus.

"My name is Dr. Galloway. Can you blink your eyes for me?"

A white blur moves in front of the blue figure, and with all the effort I can muster, I close and reopen my eyes.

"Blink once for no and twice for yes; can you hear me?"

I close my eyes, open, close, and open them again, yes.

"Do you know your name?"

I blink twice, *yes*, and I slur, "Daniel."

"Daniel?" the doctor asks.

I blink twice more for yes and slur the same.

CHAPTER 22

I am responsive

"Good morning, Daniel," the doctor says from the foot of the bed.

"Where am I?" I ask.

"You are in the ICU at Saint Joseph's Hospital," Dr. Galloway says.

"My body hurts," I say, trying to move my hands.

"You are going to have to take it slow, Daniel. You were in a coma for just over a week, and you've been in varying stages of consciousness since then," the doctor says.

I try to focus on his face but find my eyes wanting to close.

"Do you remember where you live?" he asks.

It seems like something that I should know, but I don't. "I can't remember."

"It's okay. You are probably going to feel a little disorientated for a while," he says.

"I need you to try and follow my finger," he says and moves a finger in front of my face from side to side. I do as he asks.

"The recovery process varies; it can take weeks or, like in your case, it can take months. You are one of a very low percentage of people that show signs of a full recovery after more than a couple days in a coma," he says.

"Months? I thought I was in a coma for a week."

"You were in a coma for eight days, but you have been here in the ICU for ... " He looks at his clip board. "just over six weeks."

"I was walking, and everything was blue." My mind is racing, and I have to close my eyes to try and rearrange the thoughts, but I can't decipher between dreams or memories.

"I," I start, "What happened to me?"

"You overdosed on sleeping pills, and you collapsed in the street," the doctor says.

"Overdosed? I remember people standing around me looking down at me, then a bright flash," I say and struggle to remember anything else before it.

"You didn't have a wallet or ID on your person when you were brought in, and most of the information on the label of the pill bottle had been scratched away. We had no way of contacting your family to let them know you were here," he says.

I stare at him. "I can't remember my family."

"Like I said, recovery can be a slow process. It may take some time for your memory to return," the doctor says.

"If I tried to kill myself, maybe it's better if it doesn't," I say.

The doctor is staring at the clipboard, which I assume is his way of avoiding eye contact, as he sidesteps my comment. "There were some issues regarding your blood work that we are going to have to discuss, Daniel, but right now you are stable. I'm going to put you in touch with a counselor, to help you through the process."

"Was I paralyzed?" I ask, remembering a distant feeling of being pinned or held down.

"Just try to relax." Dr. Galloway walks to the side of the bed. "I'll have someone come in and talk to you."

"About why I tried to kill myself?" I ask.

"We have to make sure that when you are ready to leave that you are not going to try and hurt yourself again," he says.

For some reason, it bothers me that he says hurt instead of kill, but I let it go.

"Will my memory return?" I ask.

"I think it will, Daniel, and I think that you should try and prepare yourself for whatever it was that made you want to end your life," he says.

"What? How do I do that?" I try to sit up and my body hurts. I let out a groan.

"Try to take it easy. Your muscles are going to be weak; try to keep your movements slow and gentle at first until you get used to it," he says.

"It feels like I've been in a coma for years," I say.

"It's going to take a while for everything to adjust, Daniel, just take it slow and please speak to the counselor when he or she comes," he says.

"Okay," I say.

I begin to stretch and rotate my ankles, then my wrists and hands. I open up my hands, with my fingers splayed out, and it seems somehow familiar, like déjà vu, a ghost of my forgotten past.

CHAPTER 23

I am agitated

"Hello, Daniel, my name is Susan Harding, and I represent the department of mental health," she says.
"Hi." I sit up against my pillow to see her.
"Dr. Galloway has asked me to come and speak to you," she says.
I don't like the tone or slowed pace in which she speaks and feel like the conversation is going to be laborious. I wait for her to continue.
"Dr. Galloway tells me that you tried to end your own life, Daniel, is this true?" she asks.
"I know less about it than he does; I don't remember it," I say.
"How do you feel now, Daniel? Are you thinking about harming yourself again?" she says, clearly enunciating every syllable.
"I feel tired," I say in the same manner.
"You seem agitated, Daniel, do you remember being on any kind of medication?" she asks.
"I am agitated, and I don't remember anything before waking up here, which is one of the reasons that I am agitated," I say.
"I'm just trying to find out if you know the reason that you tried to harm yourself, Daniel," she says.
"If, and when, you find out why I tried to *kill* myself, then be sure to let me know too because I don't have a clue," I say.
"Okay, Daniel, calm down, I'm just trying to help," she says.

"I'm sorry, I don't know where that came from." I fidget in my bed and I'm trying to remember something, anything.

"Does your family have a history of, or have you been diagnosed with," she starts and I cut her off.

"I don't know anything. I don't remember anything," I reply.

She tilts her head and feigns a sympathetic smile.

"Okay, I'll ask Doctor Galloway to reschedule a visit when you are ready," she says.

"Thank you," I say.

"If anything comes back, or you just want to talk, then have Doctor Galloway contact me," she says.

"Okay. I will. I'm sorry that I snapped, and I'm sorry that I can't answer your questions," I say, "I wish I could."

"It's okay, Daniel. If anything starts to come back, then maybe you could write it down for our next visit," she says.

"Okay, I will," I say.

"Goodbye," she says.

"Bye," I say.

A woman dressed in blue scrubs walks in and says, "Good morning, Daniel, how are you feeling today?"

"Can I have a pen and paper?" I ask.

She studies me for a second.

"I'm not going to kill myself with it," I say.

She shoots a disapproving glance.

"Sorry, it's so I can write things down, if, and when, I remember them," I say.

"I will see if it's okay, sir," she says.

***

She comes back in with a felt tip pen and a couple sheets of notepaper and hands them to me.

I write on the notepaper, *My name is Daniel. I tried to kill myself. I've been in the hospital for almost two months, and nobody has come to see me. Was anyone looking for me? Did anyone care that I was gone?*

CHAPTER 24

I am the big bad wolf

As if flicking rapidly through television channels, partial memories flash behind my eyes. I am running on a school track, then I'm sitting in a library in detention. I'm sitting cross-legged on the dirt in front of a mud hut in the blistering hot sun. I am playing chess with a skinny kid wearing thick glasses.

I'm on a school playground with other kids, and a ball hits me in the face. The sun is in my eyes and then blotted out by a large shape that says, "Nice catch, nerd."

"I think I'm starting to remember something," I say.

"That's good; try not to force it, just let it come in its own time," Dr. Galloway says.

I write down the details of the images or memories as they occur. My head begins to ring with pain and I tell the doctor this.

"I'll have the nurse bring you something for the pain," he says.

Images dance frantically in my mind, then slow to reveal the silhouette of a woman sitting by a window; her hair is up, and the profile of her face and long slender neck make my heart skip and my chest tighten.

As I move closer, the silhouette morphs, and I am back on the school grounds. I hear another voice repeat, "Nice catch, nerd."

The large shadowed figure in front of me says, "What are you going to do, big bad wolf? Blow me?"

I am sitting at a desk with a newspaper open in front of me. There is a full-page article entitled, "Elevator to Heaven," about an elderly woman that died in a hospital elevator after it stopped between floors and remained there for two hours. It says that the family is suing the hospital for improperly maintaining its facilities. I cut out the article and pin it to the corkboard on the wall behind the desk. All of the various newspaper and magazine articles pinned to the board seem to have been written by the same person—D. Wolfe.

There are papers everywhere, and a nearly empty bottle of vodka sits on the desk next to a laptop computer. I am watching the small vertical line flash on and off, waiting for me to type.

Boxes start to appear and expand from the right hand side of the screen, and letters start moving from one side to the other, as I look at the screen. The letters stack to the left in what looks like nonsense.

I pick up the bottle of vodka and finish it before throwing it at the wall. It doesn't break, but bounces with a hollow thud.

I am standing in front of a mirror in the bathroom, and the man that stares back at me is crying. His eyes are brown and framed by red, and his face is thin and gaunt, shadowed by a couple days stubble that emphasizes a dimpled chin. His hair is short and messy but falls with a natural parting to one side. He brings cupped hands up to his face and splashes cold water that I can feel on my face.

I open my eyes and I see the nurse. "Excuse me?"

"Yes, sir, what do you need?" she says.

"Can I have a mirror?" I ask.

"There is a mirror in the bathroom, sir, but you're not supposed to get out of bed until your catheter and everything else are taken out," she says.

"When will that be?"

"I will ask the doctor for you, sir," she says.

"Thank you."

I add to my notes, *Daniel Wolfe? Journalist?*

***

An hour or so later, a large woman enters the room and begins to remove everything that is attached to me, other than the IV line. It is unpleasant, and I find myself unable to look her in the eyes during the process. When she leaves the room, I turn my body and swing my legs down off the bed. I step down and my legs quiver and buckle, collapsing me to my knees. I pull myself up to standing and steady myself with the bed rail and IV stand. After taking a minute for the pins and needles to subside, I hobble and shuffle toward the bathroom using the IV stand as a makeshift walking staff. There is a blue curtain that hangs to within two feet of the floor, which I draw back before entering. I turn and face the mirror, and a bearded version of the man from my memory stares back at me.

"Hello, Daniel," we say in unison.

CHAPTER 25

I am in limbo

Lying in a hospital bed for nearly two months has really taken its toll on my body. I can't make it more than a block without having to stop. I catch my breath, and in the reflection of a store window, I see a bearded man all hunched over with his hands pressed against his thighs and looking about to keel over. I snigger a little to myself at the stereotypical jeans and tweed jacket outfit that I'm wearing. I *look* like a journalist or a science professor.

I am thinking that sneaking out of the hospital without being discharged may not have been a great idea, but after a week of being fully conscious, just lying there and having to talk to the counselor about things that I still don't remember, I was desperate to get out of there. I don't have a plan, money, or ID. I don't know where I live or where I work. I was hoping that after leaving the hospital, I would instinctively know where to go and that seeing something familiar would kick-start my memory, but nothing has yet. The memories that have come back on their own are partial and disjointed.

My legs still feel weak, and my lungs and chest are tight. I make my way to a park bench and slouch down on it. I pull out the notes that I made in the hospital and read the name, *Daniel Wolfe*.

There is a public phone booth outside of a pub on the corner a few streets down. I make my way there, hoping that there is a phonebook so I can look myself up, but when I get there, the phone has only half a receiver and a chain that hangs empty, where I assume a phonebook once hung. I rest a second then enter the pub.

"Excuse me, do you have a phonebook?" I say from the end of the bar.

"Hold on a second, dear, I'll be right with you," the woman says through bright red lips.

I sit and wait on one of the bar stools, ignoring a few strange glances from people that look like they've been here for a while.

"Sorry, what can I get you, dear?" She turns to me and her oversized gold earrings reflect all the colors of the neon beer signs through stiffened blonde curls that look like they would shatter if touched.

"Do you have a phonebook?" I ask.

She reaches back, grabs a phonebook and puts it on the bar in front of me, then returns to the drunk who is tapping his empty glass on the bar. I open the book, thumb through the pages, and run my finger down the names. I have pen and paper poised, ready to copy down all the information for every Wolfe that is listed when the woman behind the bar comes back and says with a well-practiced smile, "Just take the page hon, nobody uses those anymore."

"Oh, okay, thanks, I really appreciate it," I say.

"Looking for your relatives?" She bends down to put away the clean glasses.

Her bleached blonde curls hang parallel to the floor, seemingly defying the laws of physics, and through a smirk, I say, "I'm trying to find out where I live."

She frowns and says, "Most people forget where they live on the way out of here, not on the way in."

"I was in a coma; I got out of hospital today. My memory is still a little *hazy*."

"Really?" She stops what she is doing and regards me like a riddle.

I nod.

"Wow, and I thought I had problems. You want a drink?" she asks.

"I have no wallet, no money, and no ID," I say and pull the lining from my pocket as if she needs proof.

"I'm pretty sure you're old enough to drink," She winks at me. "It's on me; what'll it be?"

"I ... " The image of the vodka bottle projectile pops into my mind. "Vodka?"

"You don't sound too sure," she says with a grin.

"I'm not," I say.

"Vodka it is, neat?" she asks and pulls a bottle from a shelf on the back wall.

"I guess so," I say.

She puts the glass down in front of me, pours the clear liquid, and asks, "So what *do* you remember?"

"My name, and a few disjointed childhood memories, not much," I say.

"So are you just going to call all of those numbers until someone recognizes you?" She replaces the bottle.

"I was thinking about maybe going to some of the addresses listed, to see if it jogs anything."

"That sounds like a lot of walking around," she says raising one eyebrow.

"I think I'm a journalist for a magazine, or newspaper, or something," I say.

"You look like a journalist," she says with a bright red smirk.

I chuckle, "That's what I thought when I caught my reflection." I sip from the glass and wince a little.

"You want me to add coke?" she asks, empathizing with a subtle imitation wince of her own.

"Sure, thanks."

"My name's Barb," she says.

"I'm Daniel."

"You could call around the local newspapers to see which one you work at?" She sets the mixed drink back down in front of me.

"That's a good idea."

"Have you tried looking yourself up online?" she asks.

"No, I got out of hospital about an hour ago," I say and gingerly sip from the glass.

"Let me just serve Gerry, then I'll look you up on my phone," she says and rushes away.

I say, "Thanks, Barb."

"You're welcome, hon," she says and pours another pint for the bearded old guy at the other end of the bar.

She pulls her phone from her bag and returns to me. "Daniel what?"

"Daniel Wolfe," I say.

She types it in and starts scrolling through the results. "There are a lot of people by that name. I'll do an image search. That might be easier."

She scrolls through page after page and then says, "I think that's you."

I look at the photo. It is a black and white headshot.

"The photo is kind of small, but it looks like you." She clicks on it and regards it for a second. "Yeah, it's you, but your name isn't Daniel."

"What?" I say.

"It's David," she says.

"David Wolfe?" I say it out loud.

I say it again, "David Wolfe," hoping that it will clear away some of the fog but it just adds to my confusion.

"You're a writer, journalist, thirty-six years old, or at least, you were when you last updated your profile. It has some of your articles on here too. 'Super hero or superfluous heroism.' A passer-by intervened when he saw a woman and a man arguing. The argument between the woman and her boyfriend turned violent, and the Good Samaritan, Karl Wallace, stepped in to protect her. The woman refused to give a statement to police, and Mr. Wallace was arrested for restraining the boyfriend; however, charges have since been dropped after security video from a nearby gas station corroborated Mr. Wallace's initial statement to police."

"What else does it say *about me*?" I ask.

"It says that you are a former staff writer for *Hierarchy Magazine*, now a freelance journalist, your work has been published by all the newspapers," she says.

"Does it have an address or anything?" I ask.

"It has your e-mail, David-Wolfe-@-journalist-profile-dot-com and your phone number," she says.

"Would you mind calling the number?" I ask.

"Sure." She dials the number. "It's your voice, and your mailbox is full."

I take a sip of my drink. "So how can I go about finding out where I live?"

"Can I get another, please, Barb?" says a guy wearing a cowboy hat, standing at the bar with his empty glass.

"Be right with you, hon," she says and turns to me, "I'll be right back."

I pick up her phone and look at my profile. I notice the date on the most recent articles. They are all more than three years old, which coincides with the *last updated* heading, which is also three years old, which makes me thirty-nine years old.

I write down the contact information for all the newspapers and magazines associated with the articles. Barb returns, and I ask if I can make a couple calls to the newspaper on her phone.

"Sure, hon, good luck," she says.

I call the first number I have written down, the articles editor for Hierarchy Magazine. A woman answers, "Hierarchy Magazine, Janet speaking."

"Oh, hi, Janet. I'm calling on behalf of David Wolfe," I say.

"Okay, what can I do for you?" she pauses.

"Daniel," I fill in the space.

"What can I do for you, Daniel?" she says.

"I am just calling around to all of Mr. Wolfe's regular publishers to make sure they have his current contact information on file. I am Mr. Wolfe's personal assistant; he moved recently, and I've been chasing and cancelling checks that have gone to his old address. It's been a nightmare, Janet," I say.

"Okay, let me put you through to Admin, Daniel, just a sec," she says.

It rings again, and another woman picks up, "Hierarchy Magazine, Amy speaking."

I repeat my pitch, and she tells me to hold while she checks the records for my contact information. Barb looks at me and I give her the thumbs up. When Amy comes back onto the phone, she reads off the information, and I write down the address. I tell her that the information is correct, not to worry, and thanks for her time.

"I got an address," I say to Barb.

"Do you want another drink?" she asks.

"No, I think I should probably go. I'll come back and pay you for the drink though," I say.

"Alright, hon," she says.

"See you, Barb. Thanks for all of your help."

"Here's my number; call me if you need anything," she says and writes her phone number down on the paper in front of me.

I smile at her. "I will."

"Do you want me to look up the address on my phone before you go?" she asks.

"That would be great," I say.

She writes the directions down on the paper in front of me, and we say goodbye.

CHAPTER 26

I am home

I push the building manager button, and an elderly female voice answers, "Hello?"

"Hi, it's David, from apartment 604; I've misplaced my keys. Can someone let me in?" I say.

"Hold on a minute," her voice crackles when she speaks, and I can't tell if it is because of the intercom or her age.

A couple minutes pass, and then an older woman comes slowly to the door and opens it.

"David. I haven't seen you for ages," she says in the same crackly tone.

"I was in the hospital; I was let out this morning," I say.

"Hospital? Are you okay?" She looks up at me like she is regarding a giant.

"I hit my head or something; I lost my memory and my keys," I tell her, avoiding eye contact as I do so.

"You lost your memory?" she asks and I'm not certain if she is checking to make sure that she heard me correctly or if she wants me to elaborate.

"It's starting to come back, I think," I say.

"Well, at least you remembered where you live," she replies with a smile that fits perfectly between all of the lines on her face, a task that would seemingly take a lifetime of rehearsal to accomplish.

I smile as an automatic response. "Can you let me into my apartment?"

"No problem, dear. Did you report your keys missing?" She turns and starts slowly toward the elevators.

"No. I wanted to check the apartment to see if they were in there first," I say.

"Okay, well, if they're not, I will cut you another set, but you will have to report them missing if your door fob is on your keys," she says.

"I will," I say.

We wait for the elevator in silence. I have no idea who she is, other than the building manager, but she is staring at me like she is expecting conversation. I pretend like I'm checking my pockets for something, even though I know that they are all empty save for the folded paper containing my notes.

The elevator door opens, and I have to stop the door from closing on her multiple times as I wait for her to shuffle inside. I join her in the elevator, push six, and the doors close. I keep my eyes on the buttons, but out of my peripheral vision, I can see her staring at the side of my face.

We trade a couple uncomfortable smiles as the door opens to the sixth floor, and I wait for her to exit the elevator and follow her to the door marked 604. I try desperately to remember her name, or anything at all about her, but my mind is blank.

She pulls a large set of keys from her cardigan pocket and fumbles through them with trembling hands for what seems like an hour before saying, "I think it's this one," and tries it in the lock.

I am both relieved and grateful when I hear the lock open. "There you go, dear," she says.

"Thank you so much. I will let you know if I find my keys," I say.

"You're welcome, dear," she says and begins the long shuffle back to the elevator.

I don't feel good about leaving her out in the hallway, but I walk into the apartment and close the door quietly behind me.

The apartment is fairly small. There are two doors leading off from the main room, and a fake granite-looking laminate breakfast bar separates the kitchen from the living room. The living room has in it an old brown couch, a non-matching reclining leather chair, coffee table with a cup and a few magazines spread over it, several large stacks of books on the floor against the far wall, and a desk with a laptop computer. Fixed to the wall behind the desk is the corkboard from my memory with countless articles pinned to it. I move toward the laptop and rub the track pad, but nothing happens. I hit the power button and still nothing. I unwrap the charger sitting next to it, plug it into the laptop and the wall socket, and continue my tour of the apartment.

Behind door number one is a bedroom. The bed is unmade, and there is a pile of clothes in the corner. I enter and look through the small closet that contains a number of suit jackets and slacks. Apart from a selection of tweed, everything else is plain black, grey, or brown.

I pull open the drawers of the dresser one-by-one, socks and underwear, undershirts and T-shirts, and the bottom drawer contains folded brown and grey corduroys and blue jeans. On the bedside table, there is a lamp, a thick book by Noam Chomsky, and a set of keys with plastic fob attached.

I leave the bedroom and check the kitchen to see if there is anything I can eat. There are a few sticky notes on the fridge with various names and numbers, and a few notes held to the fridge under magnets. I open the fridge and look through its contents. There are spoiled greens in the crisper, and bottles of water and condiments in the door. I open the cupboards, rummage through the various cans of soup, and pull out beef lentil. I read the cooking instructions on the back of the can while I search the drawers and cupboards for a can opener and pot.

After setting the pot and its contents on the burner, I continue my tour. Behind door number two is a small 70s-style bathroom with an off-white sink, square wall cabinet with mirrored door, toilet, bathtub and shower combined, and a few toiletries. I stand in front of the mirror and stare at my reflection. His face still seems foreign to me.

"Hi, my name's David," I say, "I think."

I try a more confident tone. "David Wolfe, journalist."

I remember crying in front of this mirror, but I don't remember why. I open the cabinet and there are shelves filled with pill bottles—Doxepin, Lisinopril, Alprenolol, and many others that I cannot pronounce. I pick up the Doxepin and read the label. Printed on the sticker it says, *take 2 at least 3 hours after last meal and 30 minutes before bedtime. David R. Wolfe. Dr. Hossieni.* I take the pill bottle with me and set it next to the laptop. I push the power button and it whirs and chimes.

While I wait for the computer to boot up, I return to the kitchen and pull the pot off the burner before turning it off. I look for a spoon and a bowl and eventually just pour the contents into a mug that I take from the sink.

I leave the soup to cool while I open up the Internet browser on the laptop. I type Doxepin into the search engine and find out that it is a type of sleeping pill, probably the type that I tried to kill myself with. I type in David Wolfe, open my profile page, and begin to read the articles as I sip from the mug.

By the time I have finished what I can manage of the soup, there is a sharp pain working its way from eyes, up over my head, and I assume that it is from staring at the computer screen. I return to the bathroom and search through the pills until I find Aspirin, pop the cap, and take two with a mouthful of water from the tap.

I walk back into the living room, sit in the leather chair, pull the lever, and recline into an almost lying down position before closing my eyes, waiting for the headache to subside.

CHAPTER 27

I am heart-broken

I went back to the pub to see Barb after finding my wallet in the pocket of a pair of jeans on my bedroom floor. I told her that I had gone there to settle my bill, but the real reason was that I don't really know anyone else.

I've been having strange dreams since coming out of the coma, and I don't know who she is, but she has been in almost all of them. The pale-skinned nurse that makes my heart ache. I'm wondering if she is an old girlfriend or just someone that I knew, but I haven't seen her in any of the photographs on my laptop.

I'm starting to remember certain people and places. The kid who threw the ball in my face was named McGuire. I received almost daily punishment from him and his jock friends during high school. It would start with, "What time is it, Mr. Wolfe?" then someone would add, "Time to hand over your lunch money," or, "Time for you to run, Davey boy." *I hated being called Davey boy.*

I remember Janet, the editor from Hierarchy Magazine. According to my journalist profile, I haven't worked for that magazine for over six years, which is probably why she didn't seem to remember my name when I spoke to her on the phone.

***

I am sitting on my chair in the reclined position, and I'm going through my phone. I have to scroll back through text messages to find context and meaning behind conversations, a couple words in-turn, between people that I do not know and me. Almost all of the messages are work related, editors and such, and as I look at the dates, most of the text messages are over two, and even three years old. I check my voice mail, and there are several hang-ups and three messages from a man named Harry Maddox asking for me to call him back. There was a call from another journalist named Christopher Denis who wanted to know if I could put him in touch with the photographer that shot a piece I did a few years back on the homeless of the lower east side.

I scroll through the contacts in my phone and three-quarters of them are editors, photographers, journalists, and accounts departments for newspapers. Of the few contacts that don't have work information listed in their contact, there is Aunt Sarah, Gareth Peters, and Mom, and although I can easily ascertain by name the relationship between myself, Mom, and Aunt Sarah, I would still have nothing to say to either of them if I called. I would not want to admit to my mother that I don't know who she is, and I don't want to worry her that her son tried to kill himself and just got out of the hospital.

Reading *Mom* on my phone overwhelms me with guilt and shame for having tried to commit suicide, and I begin to wonder again, what kind of person I must have been, to not care about Mom or Aunt Sarah, or Gareth Peters, whoever that is. *I tried to kill myself, knowing that I would leave these people behind to mourn my death.* Then I remember that I am the kind of person who is not looked for, or visited in the hospital, the kind of person that hasn't received a call from his mother in years, judging by the list of received calls that mostly occurred almost three years ago.

Although I tried to kill myself only two months ago, my life seems to have ended almost three years ago. I haven't updated my profile, published any articles, or kept in touch with anyone for three years. What happened that made everyone stop calling, and that made me stop working. I remember the vodka, the papers thrown everywhere, the launching of the bottle that did not break, and I glance over at the dent at the bottom of the wall. I remember crying in the mirror, and I remember grabbing the pills.

I retrieve an arm full of the pill bottles from the bathroom cabinet, before returning to my laptop and typing the name of the first bottle into the search bar. I continue to search all of the names one-by-one and read the description of each. Angiotensin-converting enzyme inhibitor, Beta-blockers, long-acting nitrate, calcium channel blocker, and as I figure out what they all have in common, I realize what happened three years ago that had made me cut myself off from everything and everyone. I was diagnosed with terminal heart failure.

CHAPTER 28

I am in denial

I don't know what I'm going to say. I have been holding the phone for an hour, periodically touching the screen to wake it up but not able to just press the call button, and the screen fades to black again. I spend another couple of minutes with my thumb over the call button, willing myself to call her and realize that I have touched it by accident. The screen reads, *calling Mom*, and I quickly bring the phone up to my ear.

"Sorry, the number you have dialed is no longer in service," an automated female voice says over and over.

My only other choice is to call *Aunt Sarah* and ask her how I can get in touch with Mom. I pull up her number, and with only a slight hesitation, I hit the call button.

"Hello?" a female voice answers, sounding younger than I expected.

"Aunt Sarah?"

"Is that David?" she asks.

"Yes, is that Sarah?"

"No, it's Karen," she says.

I try to play it off like an honest mistake, "Oh, you sound just like her on the phone."

"That's what everyone says," she says through a breathy laugh, "we haven't heard from you in ages."

"I know, sorry. The reason I called, I was trying to call Mom, and it said that the number I dialed is no longer in service, somehow I've only got her old number. Do you know what her new number is?" I say, hoping that it hadn't sounded as ridiculous to her as it had to me.

"Who is this?" she snaps.

"It's David."

"Is this a joke?" she says and she sounds mad.

I'm thinking that maybe there is some kind of bad blood between my mom and my aunt, and I am beginning to wish I hadn't called.

"It's not a joke, Karen, look, I'm sorry if there's something going on between you and Mom, but,"

"If you were David, then you would know that Aunt Margret has been dead for years," she snaps and hangs up.

I don't know how I feel. I don't know how I should feel. I don't remember my mother, but I just found out she's dead. My chest tightens, and there are shooting pains down one leg. I try to swallow down the lump and ignore the acid in my throat and chest. Before I realize it is happening, I hear myself crying. I know hardly anything about myself, and what little I *do* know, I don't want to believe.

CHAPTER 29

I am angry

The life that I knew almost nothing about is flooding back and falling apart all over again. I am reminded of Dr. Galloway's comment about preparing myself for when my memories start coming back. How could I prepare for this? My mother is dead; I'm assuming that my father is too, or at least there is no entry for him on my phone, and I am dying.

I remember getting the call, telling me to come in to discuss the results of the tests. I remember Dr. Hossieni giving me the bad news, and I remember laughing nervously, watching his unchanging expression as he said, "I'm sorry, David." I remember trying to drown the truth in alcohol, and instead, just trashing my apartment and shutting myself off from the world. I remember waking up on the floor clutching my chest, with the worst hangover, and my jeans soaked with urine, having been too drunk to wake up in the middle of the night. I remember reading up on the life expectancy of someone in the later stages of heart failure and launching the empty bottle at the wall. I remember cutting myself off from everything to make it easier on everybody when I died, and I remember feeling sick to my stomach from sitting around, waiting to die.

I remember taking the pills with the intention of going to sleep peacefully by the water, but at the last minute, I lost my nerve or changed my mind.

CHAPTER 30

I am bargaining

I feel completely alone. It seems that I spent three years distancing myself from people so that I could die, and now, I am sitting here alone in my apartment wishing that I had a friend to talk to. I called Gareth Peters, hoping that he was a friend, and after a few minutes managed to figure out that he runs a support group for the terminally ill that I had attended for the last time just four months ago. I didn't tell him about my suicide attempt or the coma. I just told him that I had been busy making preparations for when my time is up. He said that I should come by for the meeting, but I told him that I wasn't up to it right now, and maybe I would come by next week.

Last night, I found myself praying to God, a god that I am not sure I believe in, to let it all be a bad dream that I will wake up from. I can't get my head around what is happening; it's like I have woken up in someone else's life, with a stranger's memories. I beg of God to give me a second chance. I don't remember most of the life I led before—the life in which I must have done something wrong—something that offended God, or karma, or whatever governs such things. I feel like I am suffering the punishment for someone else's mistakes or misgivings. Maybe this has nothing to do with karma or God. Maybe there is no God, no heaven, and no hell. I am being spoon-fed the events of my life, one mouthful of déjà vu at a time.

My head and heart hurt both physically and emotionally. I am not sure which pills I am supposed to take and when. I have refused to pick up the pill bottles that are strewn across my floor, like going back on the pills will somehow make the situation real. I am still waiting for some kind of intervention, someone to call and tell me it was all an elaborate hoax, that there has been some mistake or mix up, that I am not dying.

CHAPTER 31

I am depressed

I have spent the whole morning lying on my couch with my stomach in knots, waiting for something to happen, waiting for someone to come and help me. My body is shaking like I have consumed two pots of coffee, and my mind is locked in a war between depression and anger, between crying and hating myself for it.

I want to get up, but in my mind, I am asking what the point is. My head is pounding, my mouth is dry, and I can't tell if it is hunger that I feel or if it is the same sick feeling that I've had since finding out about my heart; whichever it is, I know that food won't fix it. I make the effort to get up, pour a cup of water from the kitchen tap, and pop the cap off the Aspirin before swallowing two with a mouthful of water. I chug back the rest of the water and fill the cup again.

As I exit the kitchen, I am hit in the chest by an unseen assailant, and I drop to my knees. The invisible attacker stands heavy on my chest, digging a heel in below my collarbone, and I gasp for breath. My arm feels cold and wet, and I am expecting blood as I look and see the empty glass. I lie still and play dead, hoping that the attacker will accept my surrender and leave me breathing.

CHAPTER 32

I am accepting

"I'm dying," I say.

Barb looks at me like she's waiting for the punch line.

"It's not a joke; terminal heart failure," I say.

"Is that why you were in a coma?" Her usual service-person smile dissolves into a frown.

"Kind of. I got sick of waiting to die and tried to commit suicide with sleeping pills, but I didn't die," I tell her.

"Oh my God, I don't even know what to say," she says.

"My memory has started coming back in chunks, and the more I remember, the worse it gets," I say, "I found out that my mom is dead, I mean she died years ago, but to me, all of this has happened in the last few days."

"I can't imagine what you're going through, you poor man," she says.

"The worst thing is that I cut myself off from everybody, and I have no one to talk to about any of this. I have no friends," I say.

"You can talk to me whenever you need to, David," she says.

"Thanks, Barb. I'm sorry to dump all this on you but I was going crazy in my apartment," I say.

"So what are you going to do?" she asks.

I shake my head and lift my empty glass. "Drink. What would you do if you only had a couple years left?"

"I'd like to think that I would go to Paris, or rob a bank, or something crazy, but I would probably just sit and cry," she says.

"I don't think I'm allowed to fly, and there's no point robbing a bank; what would I do with the money? I don't need it where I'm going," I say and summon a wry smile.

She returns my smile and places another drink on the bar between us. "If I am your only friend, then you can leave it all to me."

"I'm really glad I met you, Barb, you are the nicest person I know," I say.

"Thanks," she says smiling, "but you don't know anyone else."

"So you win by default, it's still a win," I say and attempt to wink, which morphs into a wince as my chest tightens, forcing me to hold my breath until the pain dissipates.

"You alright?" she asks.

"Yeah, I'm fine. I only went back on my pills yesterday, and I'm not really sure which ones I'm supposed to be taking," I reply.

"Have you called your doctor?" she asks.

"Not yet. I guess I was just hoping that if I closed my eyes for long enough, then it would all go away," I say.

She doesn't respond, but her expression says sorry a thousand times over.

"It's okay Barb, I think that I'm only about six drinks away from the acceptance stage," I say.

"Acceptance stage? Can you accept a thing like that?" she says.

"I think acceptance is what happens when you inevitably run out of options, and have to face the fact that you are going to die, and there's not a thing you can do to change it," I say.

CHAPTER 33

I am the head vice

With my eyes closed, I can see her face, the pale-skinned nurse. I don't know her name, but she is beautiful beyond anything I can describe. It is the kind of beauty that makes me believe that there may be a god, for only the hands of a god could paint something so breathtaking. I don't know who she is, but I know that I loved her with all my heart and soul. I wish that I could remember who she is and forget everything else that I have learned about my life.

The headaches are getting progressively worse and seem to have built up a resistance to the Aspirin. I can't help but notice how rapidly I am aging. I look and feel tired and my eyes ache. The skin of my face seems thinner, almost transparent, and I am afraid to shave off the beard that conceals the dying man within it.

I am fighting emotional ambivalence and all with an almost constant feeling of nostalgia beneath, to serve as an undercoat-primer, allowing for better and wider coverage. As I hold the razor in my hand, the image of my father shaving enters my thoughts, but his face is blurred. The feeling people describe as, "Being on the tip of the tongue," when trying to think of the right words to use or when trying to think of the name of the actor from a movie, that is the way I feel about the events of my life, my fragmented past. There is always a face that I am trying to put a name to, or a blurred image that I am trying to put a face to, and the harder I think about it, the worse the pain in my head becomes.

***

As I draw the razor through the coarse hair below my cheek, I am afraid that it will drag away the skin like wet paper. I have to stretch the skin to shave the hair in the slight dip in my dimpled chin and have to go back to catch hair that I have missed a few times. Simple tasks that should be second nature seem foreign and strange. I notice a small cut on my jaw line and dab at it with tissue. As the tissue blots red, there is a memory that lingers just out of reach, like a word on the tip of my tongue. I leave a square of tissue over the cut, scoop all of the hair out of the sink and flush it down the toilet before trying to clean all of the stray hairs from around the tap.

I return to the kitchen and swallow a cocktail of pills, each with a mouthful of water. I turn one of the pill bottles in my hand as I look through the contacts on my phone for Dr. Hossieni.

"Hi, this is David Wolfe. I'd like to make an appointment with Dr. Hossieni," I say.

"Is tomorrow at 11:30 okay for you, Mr. Wolfe?" she asks.

"That's fine, thank you," I reply.

"Okay, we'll see you then," she says.

"Oh, wait, where are you located?" I say quickly before she hangs up.

She hesitates for a second and then gives me the address. I write it down and tell her thanks and I'll see her tomorrow.

On my way back into the living room, I am attacked by all of my senses simultaneously, and memories come flooding back like a thousand people shouting at once. My head feels like it is in a vice. The voices become white noise, the pictures blur, and everything is replaced by a searing pain and a high-pitched squeal as the vice tightens turn by turn. My chest joins the melee against me, and I drop to my knees, trying to catch my breath, then there is silence.

I stand up and the room is black. The furniture and objects in the room are a dark blue, and as I back away from the frozen orange figure on its knees in front of me, I am reminded in an instant of everything before I found David's lifeless body. I stare down at what looks like liquid fire inside the glass figurine in front of me. I drop to my knees, and the pain grips my head, dragging me to the floor.

CHAPTER 34

I am symbiotic

I am sitting at the laptop. Once again, I am looking up my own name, trying to find out what happened to me, but this time it is not David Wolfe that I am searching for, it is Daniel Stockholm.

There are hundreds of search results. I open one of the pages, and it is a full-page news article regarding the death of Daniel Stockholm and the resulting investigation into the actions of palliative care aid Marcus Salt.

" ... The death of Daniel Stockholm has brought forth controversial talks over the issues regarding passive euthanasia, although the nature of the 'assisted' death of twenty-four year old 'Danny,' the 'persistent vegetative state' heir to the Stockholm fortune, was anything but passive ... "

" ... Marcus Salt, one of Danny's caregivers, remains in police custody after launching Danny's ventilator through the window, leaving two other caregivers shocked, devastated, and unable to help Danny who was reliant on supplied air from the machine ... "

" ... Marcus Salt collapsed almost immediately after the incident and is claiming that he has no recollection of the events before or after. Doctors have confirmed that the cause of collapse was a grand mal seizure ... "

" ... Over the days previous to the incident, two other members of the staff experienced grand mal seizures like the one Mr. Salt suffered after 'unplugging' Danny ... "

" ... Antonio Romero, the family's long-time cook and friend was hospitalized after suffering a similar collapse just days prior to the incident and says that he also has no recollection of the events immediately prior to his collapse, right up until he woke up in the hospital. Another member of the cleaning staff also suffered a collapse in the same week due to a grand mal seizure and was hospitalized for three days but has refused to talk with reporters ... "

" ... Marcus Salt is currently undergoing psychological evaluation, and his lawyer has said that he is willing to take a polygraph test, which he is certain, will show that his client was operating under 'diminished capacity,' which some have speculated is a move toward claiming temporary insanity due to medical reasons. So far, a cause for the series of grand mal seizures has not been found ... "

" ... It is still unclear as to the direction that the prosecution will take, but there are laws governing against the passive euthanasia of persistent vegetative state patients, and there is still talk of a murder or lesser manslaughter charge ... "

" ... Active or passive euthanasia to a non-consensual patient is considered as intentional homicide, and not assisted suicide, or self-determination. If it is proved that Marcus Salt was unaware of his actions during the incident, then the charge will probably be dropped to the lesser charge of manslaughter in the absence of malice or premeditation. Although, there are reports that claim that Mr. Salt said goodbye to both Cassandra Mathews, the nurse who was in charge of Daniel's live-in care, and Anna Statham, the aunt and voluntary caregiver of Daniel, prior to the incident. There are also reports that Marcus said goodbye to Daniel before unplugging him ... "

" ... This high profile case may turn into a very complicated battle of laws and loopholes versus ethics and opinion ... "

My skin crawls, or more accurately, David's skin crawls, as I read through the various articles detailing my life and my death. The name under the heading of one of the articles is Christopher Dennis, the journalist who left a message on my phone. I was Daniel Stockholm and I am dead. I am David Wolfe and I am dying.

***

I look at the clock in the corner of the screen, and, judging from the directions on my phone, it is almost time to leave for my appointment with Dr. Hossieni.

I know now that I am not David Wolfe, but they are his memories that are returning to me. My own memories came back the instant I left his body and have stayed with me since. I am thinking that I should try to limit my interaction with any of David's family or friends. He made the choice to leave this world, and I have hijacked his body. I am the tapeworm, a symbiotic life form that lives inside another, survives on another.

I want to respect David's wish to die, but if I leave his body, I will be stuck once again in limbo. I am beginning to wonder if there is such a thing as death. My body is dead, but I have seen no god or heaven, and the afterlife, it seems, is just a timeless version of this one.

CHAPTER 35

I am the lamb in Wolfe's skin

"How are you feeling, David?" Dr. Hossieni asks.

It makes me cringe a little inside when he says David, like somehow the simple use of his name exposes me as counterfeit.

"I tried to commit suicide," I say.

The doctor rubs the side of his face, and I let him off the hook for a response that is taking a long time to formulate behind the deer-caught-in-headlights expression slapped on his face.

"I was in a coma for eight days and in the hospital for almost two months," I say, "I lost my memory, and it's just started coming back in waves."

"Do you remember anything about your condition, David?" he says.

I nod. "I know that I'm dying, but I don't remember what pills I'm supposed to take and when. That's why I'm here."

He opens the folder on his desk, takes a piece of paper out, and begins to write.

"These are the medications that you need to take, David, do you still have all of these?" he asks and slides the paper to me.

"I have a whole pile of bottles at my apartment," I say.

"Those are the ones that you *need* to take; just follow the instructions on the bottle," he says, "Have you been taking the Digoxin?"

"I don't know which ones I've been taking or which ones I am missing," I reply.

"The Digoxin will help manage some of your symptoms. You need to take all of your regular medications if you want to maintain any kind of normal activity, David," he says.

"How long do I have?" I say.

In spite of his seemingly curt nature, he manages to skirt around the answer for around five minutes with misdirection like "with adequate treatment," and, "with a healthy diet and subtle lifestyle," and, "some people live as long as."

"A year? Two years?" I cut him off.

He nods. "but there is a chance it could be much longer."

"Or shorter?" I ask.

He nods again and closes my file.

"Why didn't they tell me about my heart at the hospital?" I ask.

"I'm not sure, David, I was not informed that you were in the hospital until now," he says.

I look over the pill schedule that he has written out, and it looks like a pharmacist's shopping list.

"In your condition, coming off of your pills for more than a day or two could prove fatal," he says.

"I was in the hospital for almost two months without pills," I say.

"I guarantee that your condition was being monitored and stabilized through medication, David, or we would not be having this conversation," he says with a hint of condescension.

He hands me a prescription so long that I wonder if it could be filled in time to save my life if I were to run out.

"If you have any more questions about the medication, then call me," he says and writes something on the back of his business card before handing it to me.

"Thank you," I say.

"Visit the website on the back of my card; there's all kinds of information about dietary needs, exercise requirements and restrictions, and there is number for the heart health helpline you can call." He stands up and offers his hand out to shake.

I shake his hand and walk out of his office.

CHAPTER 36

I am a stranger

I know that I shouldn't answer; I should just let it ring, but even as I am thinking this, I pick up the phone and hit answer call.

"Hello?"

"David?" a male voice says.

"Yes, this is David, who is this?"

"It's Harry," he says.

I recognize his voice from my messages. "How are you?"

"I'm about the same, how are you?" he says, and there is an urgency in his tone.

"I'm okay. When was the last time we talked, Harry?" I'm hoping that he will let me know who he is and how we know each other without me having to ask and risk offending him.

"It's been four months, David, why haven't you picked up your phone or gone to any of the meetings? I was worried about you," he says.

I'm thinking about the awkward silence during the elevator ride with the building manager and breathe a sigh through my nose.

"This is going to sound a little strange, Harry; I was in the hospital. I was in a coma for eight days, and when I came out of it, I couldn't remember anything. I couldn't even remember who I was at first," I say.

"Hospital? Are you okay?" he asks.

"I'm okay."

There is a small pause, and then Harry says, "Do you know who I am?"

"I'm sorry, Harry, I don't."

"We met at the support group for," he hesitates.

"I know that I'm dying, Harry, it's okay."

"We've been friends for two years," he says.

"It's nice to know that I had a friend; I was beginning to wonder."

His voice breaks a little. "I thought that maybe you had …"

I cut him off before he has a chance to finish. "It's okay, Harry, I'm fine. I guess I got my pills all mixed up and took a bad combination. I went and saw Dr. Hossieni yesterday and got him to write down my pill schedule for me."

"Did he tell you how long?" he asks.

"He said that if I keep myself relaxed and lay off the salt that I could keep going for years, three, four." I make an effort to keep my pitch optimistic.

Harry is quiet on the other end of the phone.

"Harry?"

"I'm still here. I guess when your only chance of making friends is at a group for the terminally ill, you should expect a limited time offer on friendship," he says.

I try to think of something to say, but I can't.

"Sheryl died last week, and I didn't say goodbye," he says.

"I won't leave without saying goodbye, Harry."

I can still hear him in the earpiece, but he doesn't say anything.

"Is it your heart too, Harry?"

"No, leukemia. I don't know how long I have left. They said a year. That was five years ago," he says.

"I'll come by the meeting next week, Harry, I promise."

"I just wanted to talk to you. I know that you don't remember me, but it's still good to hear your voice, David," he says.

"You too, Harry."

"Goodbye, David," he says.

"Goodbye, Harry."

CHAPTER 37

I am the common denominator

As the day progresses, I find that I become more confused, trying to untangle my childhood memories from his. Our lives have become entwined, but he no longer has any say in the authorship of what is to be the epilogue of his life. I feel an overwhelming guilt at times when I am forced to impersonate David, and to all that perceive my performance, I am indiscernible from the original, a perfect copy with all of his memories to use for reference during unavoidable interactions.

At night, I recline in his chair and let the world around me turn to stone as I leave my nest and liberate myself from his memories, begging God, karma, or fate to give me a sign to let me know if what I am doing is wrong. Each night, I expect to return to a reclined statue, locked and reluctant, but instead, he waits for me like an empty suit, or more aptly, a uniform that comes with its own expectations and responsibilities.

Is this the way it is for everyone when they die? Do they leave their shell, to wander around a frozen landscape until a new host is found? Maybe when we are ready to let go of our memories, we are allowed to move on. Maybe we are symbiotic entities by nature, needing to fuse with flesh to comprehend time and fluid physicality. Maybe, when we let go of our old lives, we are allowed to settle in a new womb, to be born once again, cleansed of our memories and of our sins.

I do not feel as though I have eluded death, and I have no delusions of grandeur or exclusivity. I am the unwilling participant in an esoteric game of which I am ignorant to the rules. I take my turn each night as I negotiate the petrified blue-black game board, expecting fate to take its turn and for me to be locked out once again. I am unsure as to whether the correct emotional response should be one of indignation or gratitude as I am allowed to return to the world and continue with a life that is not my own.

CHAPTER 38

I am the product of his environment

I'm twelve years old and hiding behind a parked car, waiting for McGuire and his entourage to pass on the other side of the street. Other kids walk past me, glancing down at me, and I am cowering and pathetic. I meet the gaze of each with a silent plea that they won't give me away. I am used to the teasing and the beatings, but if they see me and decide to toy with me for too long, I will miss my bus and have to wait an hour for the next one or walk home. In the short stories I write, I am heroic, courageous, and tough, but really, I'm just a victim. I didn't really ever have a father to teach me how to fight or stick up for myself. The heroes in my stories are as much a surrogate for the father figure that I wish I'd had instead of the one that walked out on my mom when I was a baby, as they are surrogates for me, with my skinny non-threatening frame and low self-confidence. I aspire to be more like the protagonists from the science fiction stories I read, strong, bold and unafraid, but I am weak and unable to defend myself. Not that bravery would in any way overcome the fact that McGuire is over a foot taller than me, built like a car, and always has his two friends with him, ready to chase down his prey and hold it squirming until McGuire saunters up and lays in with his fists and size eleven boots. I wonder if I ever meet my father, if I will be able to look him in the face and admit to him that I am unpopular, a coward, a weakling, and I wonder if I can tell him that all of it is his fault for not teaching me how to be a man.

CHAPTER 39

I am the product of my environment

I am twelve years old and asking my mother to tell me about Grandma Jane. She knows what I want to know, and I am expecting her to shush me or tell me that I'm too young to understand like she usually does, but instead, she tells me to sit down and gestures to an empty leather chair in her office.

"Just give me a minute while I finish this e-mail," she says.

The walls are covered with various photos of her shaking hands with people, or standing as one of the few white faces among a group of people all smiling. One of the photos is of my mother as a child standing with Grandma Jane, and behind young Hilary there is Anna with her hands clasped and her arms over Hilary's shoulders framing her smiling face.

"So what do you want to know?" she asks as if ignoring the countless times I have brought it up to her in the past.

"I want to know about Aunt Anna's scars, and about her sister," I say.

"Why do you want to know so badly?" she asks.

"I don't know, I just do," I say, not knowing if morbid curiosity is enough of a reason to have been pestering her about it, off and on, for three years, although I assume it is the same curiosity that she, as a young girl, exhibited while pestering Grandma Jane for the truth about her sister.

"You need to promise me that you are not going to upset your Aunt Anna next time you see her," she says.

"I promise," I say.

"Your grandma was helping set up a medical depository in a small village a few miles away from where Anna and her family lived, when news came that evidence of witchcraft had been found in a few of the other villages," she says.

"Were you there too?" I ask.

"Yes, but I was too young to remember any of it," she says.

I wait patiently for her to continue, afraid that if I interrupt her again, and at the wrong moment, I will have to wait another three years for the rest of the story.

"When my mother found out about the accusations of witchcraft, it was already too late to save some of the children. Anna's parents had been convinced by the pastor of the church that both Anna and her sister were possessed by the devil and performing witchcraft," she says.

"Why would a pastor say that?" I ask.

"There are some people that choose to believe in superstition, and there are some very bad people that choose to capitalize on fear and ignorance. The most powerful and successful churches were the ones whose pastors were able to detect and exorcise evil spirits and demons," she says.

"They thought that Anna was possessed by a demon?" I ask.

My mother nods. "There were seven children, two boys and five girls, including Anna and her sister."

"So what happened?" I press.

My mother sits staring through the wall of photographs for what seems like an hour before continuing in a flat, hushed tone, "They claimed that they were exorcising the demons and forced three of the children to drink acid."

My stomach churns for having made her say it out loud, but she doesn't stop; she goes on in the same monotone fashion of someone on the brink of hopelessness.

"The parents of the children were told that their children had been taken by the devil, and the men of the church tortured confessions of witchcraft and association with the devil out of each of the children that were still able to speak." I see tears well up in her eyes, but she doesn't look at me.

"One of the boys was deemed a demonic wizard and was burned. One of the girls died within days of being forced to drink acid, another a week later, and Anna's sister lasted a month before she died of her injuries." My mother is crying silently and it is as if we are no longer in the same room.

"The three that were saved, a boy and two girls, had been beaten, cut, and whipped. Anna was one of those three children that survived. Mom took Anna, her sister, and the two others to the safety of the Christian missionary compound," she says and gives in to the tears.

"They couldn't save Anna's sister, and as for the rest of them, including Anna, they remained terrified at the sight of the cross for a long time after," she sobs uncontrollably into her hands, and in my mind, the rest plays like a later memory, when I am in my chair and unable to speak, a ghost.

CHAPTER 40

I am terminal

I called Gareth Peters, who runs the support group, for the time and place of today's meeting. I promised Harry that I would go. Gareth said that it was being held in the same place as usual, the community center in the next town over.

There is a driver's license in my wallet, but no car key on my key ring, so I am assuming that I do not own a car. I'm wondering how I would handle driving, if his knowledge and skill would take over like an automatic pilot, or if the fact that I never learned to drive would impair my efforts.

I have become the sum of two parts. Sometimes, while performing routine duties, such as shaving, to which the sole privilege had previously been his, I step outside of myself, as if watching David from the other side of the glass. I have tried to separate his memories from mine, to compartmentalize our two lives, and keep them apart, but it seems that events spill from one jar to the other. Some are like oil and water, and some mix and blend, assimilating or consuming each other until I am forced to leave the shell of David at the end of each day to reset and divide.

***

I manage to pull up the bus information and route on the transit website; it says that it's less than an hour away, but I leave early just in case. There is a bus that comes down Twelfth Street that goes to the bus depot, where I am to transfer to the number twenty-three bus, which will take me the rest of the way.

***

I have to stop every couple of blocks to catch my breath, and I am thankful that I gave myself extra time for the commute. A young woman offers me her seat at the bus stop, but I refuse, thank her, and make up an excuse about running to catch the bus, to explain the excessive panting and sweating. She smiles and returns to her magazine.

The bus arrives a few minutes later, and all seating is full. I make my way toward the back as directed by the driver. As the bus pulls away, I reach for the handrail, but miss and find myself stumbling into a large man that instantly reminds me of McGuire. I apologize at once, and he goes back to staring out of the window.

I have developed an irrational fear of a bully that I have never actually met. I was teased like every kid in school, but not to the extent that David was. Suddenly, being introduced to the emotional remnants of being hunted daily, bullied, and beaten has begun to erode my self-confidence. Even after nightly separation, the fear and hopelessness that he once felt seeps in and begins to frame my own childhood memories. My mother had said on more than one occasion that if I could put myself in the shoes of the less fortunate for even one day, then perhaps my life wouldn't seem so bad; this is not what she had in mind, but she was right. Compared to growing up without a father, with a mother working two jobs to pay for a tiny rundown apartment, and being singled out by the school bully day after day, my childhood was *not* that bad. Maybe my lack of gratitude at the time was the reason that I was deemed undeserving to live out the rest of it, and why I was offered to the parasite as food.

The bus pulls into the depot, and everyone shuffles toward the doors and out, dispersing into the crowd of people waiting to get on. I turn back and look up at the sign that reads *Terminal* before it switches to *12th Street*. As I read the word, indicative of both my location and condition, my bad heart sinks.

People stand, waiting in lines, holding bags brandishing various store names. As I study the expressionless faces of the entranced commuters, I am reminded of the blank, empty eyes of Danny, sitting helpless in his chair as I removed his ventilator. I wonder if all of us take our own lives for granted, always wanting for something better and never content with what we have, unable to appreciate what we have never had to fight for, or strive for, and only feeling cheated or deprived of things unattainable.

I see the sign hanging that says *23 Park Drive* and head toward it. I buy a newspaper to break a ten for bus fare at a hole-in-the-wall newsagent, then take a seat on the bench below the sign. I flick through to the section about Marcus, which was the reason that I chose that particular newspaper. There is no information about Marcus that hasn't already been covered in various articles before, but there is a photo of Cassie and Anna. I stare at the photo, at her.

There is a small lineup of people waiting to get on the bus when I lower the paper; I don't know how long I have been waiting. I fold up my paper and join the lineup.

I get off the bus on Main Street and follow the directions, scrawled on a scrap of paper, that eventually lead me to the community center. Coffee, juice, and muffins have been laid out on a table at the back of a large room, and there is a man setting out chairs in a circle, probably Gareth Peters.

"Help yourself to coffee or juice," he says without looking up.

"Thanks," I reply and pour myself a glass of orange juice. I pull out my phone and pretend to answer a call as an excuse to leave the room and avoid any strained, awkward conversation. I'm hoping that I will remember the regulars as they come in; being early may have been a mistake.

I keep the phone pressed against the side of my head and return the odd smile of feigned recognition as people walk through the hallway and into the main room. I recognize a greying, heavyset man from several photographs on my laptop and return the phone to my pocket.

"Harry?"

He nods and smiles. "Hello, David."

I breathe a sigh and smile. "How does this work? Are they going to ask me to talk about myself?"

"Not if you don't want to," Harry says.

"I'm still not really myself." I cringe inside as I listen to the words come out.

"You'll be fine," Harry says and gestures toward the room.

I sit patiently, with an irrepressible and morbid curiosity, sizing up the latecomers and wondering what mortal affliction is killing each of them as they enter and join the circle. Of the group, some appear at least superficially healthy, as compared with their diametric opposites, those resembling the decaying remnants of past, or passed, members.

"For anyone who is here for the first time, my name is Gareth Peters, and I am a grief counselor. Some of you are dealing personally with terminal illness, and perhaps, some of you are here because you have a loved one that is dealing with terminal illness." He speaks in the manner of someone teaching a child the alphabet, and I am beginning to wonder if it is a common trait among counselors.

As I look over at Harry, secondhand emotions lubricate the flow of memory. The man sitting next to me was more than just a friend to David. He was the long forgotten hero in a child's science fiction stories, a surrogate father figure in the absence of his own.

"Are you alright, David?" Harry asks in a crackled whisper.

The last time that we sat together, I was afraid. Sitting in a room filled with dying people but afraid of dying alone, afraid of telling Harry about my plan to put an end to the waiting.

The night that I swallowed the sleeping pills, it was the thought of leaving Harry behind to mourn my death that drove me to stagger back into town. I didn't want to die without saying goodbye, without saying sorry, but it was too late. It was too late for David. I stole his life, depriving him of his chance at redemption. My gut churns, and I feel like I'm going to be sick.

"Excuse me," I manage, as I run out of the room and to the bathroom across the hallway.

I cough and spit bile into the sink, my body trying to purge itself of remorse. David's reddened face stares back at me, and I cannot fight back the guilt or tears. "I'm sorry, David."

CHAPTER 41

I am patiently waiting for virtue

I have sat in my apartment for days, thinking, waiting, and praying for answers. I have been wallowing in self-deprecation and guilt for all of what I consider to be my sins. The fate of Marcus Salt and the theft of David's life haunt every other thought, and I can hardly bare it.

The tapeworm was not the only parasite to feed off Danny. Marcus was a coldhearted, self-centered reptile, who gained from my family, but gave almost nothing in return. He was ready to let me spend the rest of my life locked in a cage, and maybe he deserves the same, but that does not change the way I feel about what I have done.

As for David, I am in part, the sum of his memories, and as such, I am privileged to every recalled emotional response prior to the non-permissive resurrection of his body, but even with such vast reference, I am uncertain of how *he* would feel about me continuing the life that at one point he had decided to abandon. I regret answering the phone call from Harry that has since led to the inheritance of David's obligation toward him.

I am waiting for intervention, for a sign, a warning, to be struck down by God, or for David to reclaim his life, but I know that I am waiting for something that will never come. I realize that we have both spent our whole lives waiting. Waiting for the return of an estranged father, waiting to be old enough to hear the story of aunt Anna, waiting for someone to save me from my chair, waiting for someone to tell me who I am, waiting to die, waiting for someone to tell me that what I am doing is wrong. So much time wasted, waiting for something.

I am able to move and communicate, and yet, I sit still and alone. For whatever reason, I have been given another chance and don't wish to wait any longer. I would have given almost everything for this opportunity, everything except my memory of her.

***

I pick up my phone and scroll through the contacts. I hit call and it rings.

"Hello?"

"Hi, Harry, are you doing anything right now?"

"Nothing in particular; is everything alright, David?"

"Everything is fine; I've just had enough of sitting in my apartment."

"What do you have in mind?" he asks.

CHAPTER 42

I am his epitaph

"Are you supposed to be drinking?" Barb says as she places our drinks down.

"I don't think one drink is going to kill us," I say with a smirk.

"It might," Harry says through a breathy laugh that compels me to join in.

"What time are you closing up, Barb?" I ask.

"Why, what are you thinking?" she asks with a smirk.

"There's no one here; why don't you join us?" I say and raise an eyebrow.

She stands there for a second. "Alright, give me a few minutes."

"I was worried that something had happened when you called," Harry says.

"I know, and that's kind of the reason I called. Why should we only get together when there's something wrong, or when things get worse? We're dying, we're not dead," I say.

Harry smiles. "You have a point, David."

Barb slides the bolt on the doors, returns to the bar, and pours herself a drink, before coming back to join us.

"Alright, so what are we talking about?" she says and takes a seat.

"Barb, this is Harry. Harry, Barb," I say.

"Hi, Harry," she says.

"Hello, Barb," Harry says.

"And for those of you coming to this support meeting for the first time, my name is David Wolfe, and I am not a grief counselor," I say.

"So now that you've remembered you have more friends, does that mean I have to share the bank robbery money?" Barb asks.

Harry frowns and I explain the joke.

"What do you want to do before you die, Harry?" I ask.

"It's a little embarrassing, but I haven't really thought about it. I've been so busy with treatment and making arrangements for when I die to even think about it," he says.

"Well, I have spent the last two days thinking about it, and the first thing that I wanted to do was see you two," I say.

"I want to go to Paris," Barb says.

"What's stopping you?" Harry asks.

"Well, money for one, and there's the bar," she says and takes a drink.

"I just don't want to have any regrets or loose ends when I die," Harry says.

I think about David, staggering back into town with the world spinning and turning before his eyes, as the sleeping pills took hold.

"I thought about what you said to me on the phone Harry," I say.

"What was that?" he asks.

"That you didn't want me to leave without saying goodbye."

Harry looks down at his drink, and Barb looks from me to Harry and back.

"If this was the last night that we were to spend together, what would you want to say?" I ask.

There is silence for a minute before Barb says, "Hold that thought while I go get us more drinks." She leaves the table.

"Since I've been out of the coma, I've done nothing but feel sorry for myself; I don't want to spend the last few years of my life just waiting to die," I say.

Harry nods slowly and with an unreadable expression.

Barb returns with more drinks.

"A toast," Harry says picking up his glass.

"To what?" Barb asks.

"A toast to the fact that we're not dead yet," he says.

Barb smiles, "How about to friends?"

"To friends," we say in unison and clink our glasses together.

"Okay, how about this? If you could give your own eulogy, what would you say?" I ask.

"Harry Maddox has left the building," he says and laughs.

"Short and sweet," Barb says and accompanies Harry's breathy laugh with a higher pitched harmony.

"What about you, David?" Barb asks.

"I only really got to know David Wolfe after he came out of his coma, but what I have learned about him over the past while is that he didn't want to leave anyone behind to mourn him. David was a good-hearted man, with a childish optimism that was almost lost and consumed by regret and self-pity. I know that the few friends that knew him best, Barb and Harry, will miss him. Barb was the kind soul that took him in as a stray dog off the street and showed him the way home, and was the one that planted the idea for him to rob the bank that got him shot down by the police in a blaze of glory," I say.

Barb chuckles and Harry smiles at me.

"And Harry Maddox was nothing short of a father figure to David in the absence of his own. He looked up to and admired Harry the way any young boy idolizes his father as he looks up at him shaving in the mirror, wanting to be just like him, and to make him proud," I say.

"I am very proud of you, David," Harry says.

"To David," Barb says and holds out her glass.

"To David," we all say again as our glasses meet.

"Alright. Barbara Saunders was a beautiful, kind woman that everybody loved and admired for her service to the community. She will be missed greatly by her movie star husband, Brad, and three beautiful children, Paris, Moonbeam, and Brad junior," she says.

"Paris and Moonbeam?" Harry asks.

"I figure that I will probably be going through a new age phase after eloping with Brad in Paris," she says as we all laugh.

"Who are you going to leave your movie-star-wife billions to?" I ask.

"Well, Brad is obviously going to get most of it, and then the rest of it will go to Paris and Moonbeam," she says, while feigning good posture.

"What about Brad junior?" Harry asks with a smirk.

"Oh yeah, I forgot about Brad junior. He can have the French villa and the Porsche," she says giggling.

"To Barb," I say and our glasses meet again as we all repeat.

"I feel like I sold myself short on my eulogy now," Harry says.

"Do you want to add to, 'Harry has left the building?'" Barb asks.

"Harry has left the building, and now that he is dead, his next door neighbor, Thomas, can take his mower back, as Harry will no longer be needing it," Harry says.

"To Harry," we say in unison, clink our glasses, and take another drink.

We continue to drink, talk, and laugh into the early morning, and I hope that the memory of this night is what will survive us when we are gone.

CHAPTER 43

I am the aggregate

I woke up with the worst hangover, a byproduct of my need for absolution. As I recall fragments of last night, I laugh out loud and wince, admonished by a throbbing headache and chastised by my aching body, for having drank so much.

I take a couple Aspirin with a glass of water as I listen back through my phone messages to find his number.

"Hello?"

"Hi, I'm looking for Christopher Dennis." My voice is coarse and I have to clear my throat.

"That's me, who's this?"

"It's David Wolfe; you called and left a message looking for Andre's phone number." I make my way back to my desk and lean on my hand.

"David, yeah thanks, but that's an old message. I managed to get his number elsewhere. I appreciate you calling back though."

"I didn't realize it was an old message; I've been out of town for a while," I say, "Hey, I read an article you wrote for the Daily on Daniel Stockholm, great piece."

"Oh thanks. I'm doing a follow up to that piece right now," he says.

"That whole thing is still going on?"

"Yeah, it's a messy situation; it'll be dragged through the courts for months," he says.

"I went to school with one of the people in that story," I lie, "Cassandra Mathews?"

"Oh, really? Small world," he says.

"What happened to her after the Stockholm place? Did she go back home?" I say in the most casual tone I can manage.

"She's working at the care home on Carol Street," he says, "you fishing for leads?"

I feign a laugh. "No, I'm retired from journalism. I've been out of the game for three years."

"You working on a novel or something?" he asks.

"No, just trying to live out the rest of my days stress free," I say and begin searching the Internet for the care home on Carol Street.

"Each to their own; early retirement would drive me crazy, or the wife would," he says, "Oh, hey, I've got to run, I have a call on the other line, but it was good speaking to you, David."

"You too, Chris, take care," I say, but I think he may have hung up halfway through.

The website says that it is a palliative care facility. I have never been there, but I recognize the name. I look through my wallet, pull out Doctor Hossieni's card, and punch in the number on my phone.

"Hello, Doctor Hossieni's office, Joy speaking, how can I help you?"

"Hi, this is David Wolfe; can I speak with Doctor Hossieni, please?" I find myself pacing and over by the books, all stacked up against the back wall. I am picturing Cassie's wide-eyed expression at the sight of David's collection of classic fiction and science fiction.

"I'm sorry, David, Doctor Hossieni is with a patient right now; is there anything I can help you with?" Joy says.

"I don't think so; can you ask him to call me back when he's available, please?" I say.

"Okay, what is it in regard to?" she asks.

"I want to know if I'm eligible for palliative care?" I browse through the various titles from Wells, Heinlein,

Vonnegut, Brin ... when I get to Orwell, I remember what the pin code is for my bankcard, and I laugh out loud, *1984*.

"David?"

"Sorry, I wasn't laughing at you," I say and put a hand to my throbbing temple.

"Can he reach you on this number?"

"Yes," I reply.

"Alright, I will pass this on to him as soon as he's finished with his patient, David. Is there anything else?"

"No, that's it, thank you," I say.

"Okay, David, have a nice day."

I see *The Chrysalids* and it brings a smile to my face. I put my phone back into my pocket and pull at the book, careful not to collapse the haphazard stack of paperbacks above it. I begin to flick through the pages, trying to find the last page that Aunt Anna had read to me, but David has already read this book, and the two cloudy memories are fused together. I'm hoping that David has forgotten how it ends, and I slip Doctor Hossieni's card between the pages at the start of chapter one.

***

I am hoping that the Aspirin will kick in at some point and allow me to accomplish everything that I have set out to do today. Certain details of David's life are still unclear. It may be, that what I am searching for is not there to be remembered, but I don't want to base my actions on assumption and risk further karmic retaliation.

I am digging through the drawers of my desk when my phone rings.

"Hello?" I say and continue searching through the stack of papers.

"Hello, David, this is Doctor Hossieni."

"Oh hi, thanks for calling me back." I attempt to gather both the stack of papers and my thoughts.

"That's no problem, David, what can I do for you?"

"I wanted to know if I'm eligible for palliative care?"

"Your condition is considered terminal, so yes," he says in the same curt manner that makes my eyes roll in their sensitive sockets.

"How do I go about admitting myself?"

"If you have a place in mind, I can call and refer you."

"I was reading up on the Statham House on Carol Street; that's where I would like to go, as soon as possible," I say staring at the web page that is still open on my browser.

"If you are sure about it, David, then I can call them today, but even if there is an opening, there will likely be a waiting period, is that okay?" he says.

"I'm sure, and the waiting period is fine; I need a little time to sort out a few things."

"Okay, David, I think that this is probably the right move for you. I will call back later and let you know if they can get you in," he says.

I thank him before we say goodbye, and I go back to sorting through the mess of papers spread out on the desk and floor. When I find what I'm looking for, I fold it and put it into my pocket before stuffing the rest back into the drawer.

CHAPTER 44

I am counseled

I cross-reference the address with the one on the letterhead and enter through an inconspicuous door that I had missed twice previously. In the foyer next to the elevator, there is a brass plaque on the wall that lists each of the conglomerate businesses. I head up in the elevator and to the office marked with its own brass plaque, *Meacham, Dwyer, and Associates, 412*.

The girl at the desk says, "Hi, can I help you?"

"I need to talk to James Carlyle," I say.

"Do you have an appointment?" she asks and clenches the chewing gum between her teeth.

"No, I just have a couple questions."

"Your name?" she asks. I can hear the saliva squeeze out from the gum between her teeth, and I am trying desperately to hide my repulsion.

"David Wolfe."

"Just take a seat, and I will see if Mr. Carlyle is available," she says.

I take a seat and open my book. The smacking mouth noises are amplified by the remnants of my hangover and drown out the first paragraph. I read it again but my brain is glass, fragile and non-porous.

***

"David?" she says.

"Yes?"

"If you want to go through to his office, he can see you right now; it's the third door on the right," she says.

I knock before entering.

"David, how are you?" the well-groomed man says from behind an oversized desk that seems to take up all of the space in his small office.

"I'm okay. Do you remember me?" I ask.

"Of course," he says and frowns.

"Would you say that you know me well?" I ask.

"Where are you going with this, David? You've been a fairly regular client for years, with one defamation or libel accusation after another," he says.

"Okay, I'm going to give you the short version just in case I'm paying by the hour," I say, "I hit my head a couple months ago and lost my memory. It's pretty well all back, but there are a few things that I can't remember, and I figured since you are my lawyer, then you might know."

"Okay, wow, I'm intrigued," he says through a smirk, without relinquishing the frown held in his brow.

"Do I have any next of kin, or a Will?"

He hesitates for a couple seconds and then says, "No mother, absent father, no siblings, no kids that I'm aware of, and no Will."

"You're sure?" I ask.

"I advised you to talk to Jocelyn, our estate planning attorney, three years ago when you were diagnosed, 'terminal,' and you refused, saying that it was pointless because you had little to give and nobody to give it to," he says as if reading from a card, "have you changed your mind?"

"No, I just didn't want to spend the college fund set aside for a kid I didn't know I had," I say through a smirk of my own.

"Nope, you're off the hook for alimony, David," he says.

"That's all I needed; do I still have to pay for a full hour?

CHAPTER 45

I am leaving

I have been running around trying to wrap up all my loose ends for a couple days. Doctor Hossieni called back and told me that there is a place for me in the care home, and that they will be ready to accept me in just a week. I found out that my medical insurance would cover most of the cost. I spoke with the building manager, whose name I now remember is Beth, or Betty to most, and arranged to have a disposal company come in and remove my furniture when I'm gone. Everything else is packed up and ready to go.

***

I called Harry on my way to the bar and told him that I would be leaving at the end of the week, and he promised to visit me after his current round of treatment.

I arrive before the bar is open as planned, so that I can just put the envelope through the letter slot, but as I'm walking away, I hear the door open and, "David?"

I turn around. "I didn't think that you'd be here," I say.

"What's this?" she says holding out the envelope, "Are you coming in?"

I follow her in, and she bolts the door behind us.

"I wasn't expecting to be here when you opened it," I say and perch on one of the barstools.

Her eyes grow wide and her mouth opens, but she doesn't say anything.

"No, not like that. I checked myself into a care home; I'm going to be living there after this week," I say.

"I thought you meant ... " she starts.

SKIN CAGE

"No, I'm okay," I say with a reassuring smile.

She looks down at the envelope. "So what is this?"

"You might as well open it."

She opens the envelope, pulls out the letter and the second smaller envelope from inside, and frowns.

"Read it," I say.

She unfolds the paper and reads aloud, "Authorities have asked for the public's help in identifying a man being sought in connection with a bank robbery that occurred on Monday. A National Trust bank located on 12th Street was robbed at approximately 10:30 a.m.. Police have not disclosed the amount of money stolen." She looks up at me with an uneasy expression.

"Keep reading," I say with a smirk.

"Customers that were in the bank during the robbery remain shocked but uninjured. The police have released images of a man in his late thirties to early forties dressed in jeans and tweed. Police are asking all passengers of the number thirty-six bus traveling east at that time to call with any information about the suspect, as this was possibly used as the getaway vehicle. As the robber stopped to catch his breath before evading police via public transit, he is rumored to have said, 'It wasn't my idea. Barb told me to do it.' Anyone with information on the identity or whereabouts of the robber or 'Barb,' seemingly the mastermind behind the crime, are asked to contact the authorities." She hesitates for a second, then begins to laugh.

"What *is* this?" she asks.

"Open the other envelope," I say.

"Your take?" she says, reading what I have written on the envelope.

She opens the envelope and the puzzled frown seems to expand on her face, her eyes go wide, and her mouth drops open. "Paris?"

"Two tickets, there and back. You can use them whenever you want, they're open-ended," I say, smiling.

"What's this?" She pulls out the check. "David?"

"Spending money; it's your take from the robbery," I say, chuckling.

"I can't take this; it's too much," she says, shaking her head.

"What am *I* going to do with it?" I say, "I have no family; you win by default, Barb."

"I don't know what to say," she says, and there are tears welling up in her eyes.

"Just come and visit me in the care home every now and then."

I flinch a little as she throws her arms around me, "Thank you, David."

This is the first time that I have been held this way by anyone since I was fifteen years old.

"Thank *you*," I say, "for helping me remember who I am and what's important."

She returns to staring at the tickets and wipes the tears away from her eyes.

"The address for the care home is on the back of the letter," I tell her.

She flips it over and reads aloud, "To friends," and begins to half-giggle, half-cry.

"I'm going to miss you, Barb," I say.

"You won't have a chance to miss me. I'll come and visit," she says.

"Okay, I'll call you when I'm settled in."

III

CHAPTER 46

I am admitted

I pay the cab driver, pull my cases out of the back of the minivan taxi, and set them down by the step. I think about telling the driver that if he is dropping his fare off at a palliative care home with boxes and suitcases, then they are probably staying, most likely dying, and he might want to lend a hand with the luggage. I don't say this, but I think it hard enough that it radiates from my glare as we make eye contact through the half-open window via the mirror on the driver's door. I pull the last of the boxes out of the back of the van, close the hatch, and with an emphasized lack of enthusiasm, I say, "Thanks for the ride."

I assume that he was expecting a bigger tip, seeing as how I don't need it anymore, but he says nothing and pulls away.

***

By the time I have carried, pushed, and slid all of my belongings through the double doors, I am dripping with sweat. My heart, pulse, and seemingly even the blood in my veins, is beating fast and hard. My mouth is dry, and the air I'm breathing seems sharp and coarse as it scrapes its way to my lungs.

I sit in a chair in the foyer and concentrate on my breathing, trying to convince my pulse to slow down. My heart thumps in my chest six, seven, times with each strained breath in, and I am unsure if the accompanying pain is real or psychosomatic. There is pressure around my eyes, and regardless of phantom or physical status, it *hurts* like hell, like shot glasses being forcefully inserted into my skull via my eye sockets. I am trying desperately to calm down, which in itself is contradictory to the task, and with every twinge, pain, pinch, and ache, I feel closer to passing out.

I stand and turn to see the ossified liquid-fire shell, burning in the blue-black, and I stare for a while at the volcanic engine at its center, responsible for the acceleration of David's inevitable end. I take a little time to prepare and ready myself for the sensory blitz and return to my shell, doing my best to stay calm and maintain a certain mental detachment as I endure the physical onslaught for what seems like hours, but is more likely minutes.

After a time, I am able to breathe deeper, as the blades and needles are pulled out slowly, one-by-one, and the bloody wounds subsequently coagulate. My heart rate slows to a pace closer to normal, and the majority of symptoms eventually subside, leaving little trace of my attacker, save for the sole sweat-drenched survivor, exhausted from the melee.

A familiar voice says, "David?"

I breathe a sigh and rub the sweat and tears from my eyes, trying to focus on the woman standing in front of me. "Anna?"

"Yes, have we met?" she asks and cocks her head to the side.

"Your name tag," I say between deep breaths.

"Are you alright?" she takes my wrist in her hand.

"I'm fine; I just need a minute," I manage.

"Do you want a glass of water?" she asks, and I nod.

She calls to a man walking past the doorway and asks for him to bring me a glass of water.

"Your last name is Statham, any relation?" I say, already knowing the answer.

"You mean the name of the facility?" she asks, "It's named after my mother."

The young man, dressed in a light blue uniform, enters the foyer with a glass of water and hands it to me. I smile and thank him before he leaves.

"Looks like you brought a lot with you, David," she says and nods toward the boxes.

"Those are my books. I thought that maybe I could just add them to your library, if you have one," I say, sipping at the water.

Her smile widens. "We do have a library, and that is very thoughtful of you, David."

"Not entirely selfless; I couldn't bear to leave them behind or for them to be discarded along with my furniture," I say.

"I'll show you to your room, David. Are you okay to walk, or do you need help?" She lets go of my wrist.

"I'm okay." I stand up and reach for my suitcases, but she tells me to leave them, and she will have someone come back for them. I follow her through the double doors at the end of the foyer and into the main room.

"This is the dayroom, David; this is where most of our residents choose to spend their days, although some prefer to stay in their private rooms, and we ask that you respect everyone's right to privacy," she says.

I scan the room for Cassie, but she's not in the room. As I meet the gaze of the residents, most smile or acknowledge me with a wave. I smile and wave back.

Anna points to a room with a large window and says, "That's the nurse's lounge; non-staff personnel are not allowed in that room, but if you need to speak with one of the nurses, then you can ask whichever member of staff is on duty, and they will relay your message."

"Okay," I say and peer through the glass at the empty room.

"At the end of this hallway is the library. This is hallway D, and your room is 117-D," she says.

"Right between the dayroom and the library; that sounds like prime real estate," I say.

She turns and smiles. "All the rooms are pretty much the same, but if there is anything that you want to add or if there is anything you need, then feel free to ask."

"Thank you," I say and follow her to room 117.

She opens the door and we walk inside. "The facility is non-smoking; if you do smoke, then you have to go into the garden behind the house. There are designated smoking areas, and one of the members of staff will help you out there if you need it."

"I don't smoke. The room is nicer than my apartment," I say as I look around the room, "Do the rooms have cable and Internet?"

"Yes, all of the rooms have cable and Internet connection," she replies.

"This place is great," I say.

"If you have any problems with any of the other residents, then please let a member of staff know, and we will deal with the issue. There are residents here that have some mental issues, so be patient with them. We house the high-maintenance residents in C wing, and the ones that can, rarely use either dayroom, but if and when they do, just try to treat them with the same respect that you would show to anyone else," she says.

"Okay, I will," I say.

"There is a copy of the orientation plan on your bedside table, and someone will be along shortly with all of your admission paperwork. If you wouldn't mind taking the time to read through the orientation plan, while I have someone bring your belongings to you, that would be wonderful," she says and gestures toward the stack of stapled paper.

"Thank you, Anna," I say.

"You're very welcome, David, it's a pleasure to meet you," she says.

I take her extended hand in both of mine. "It's a pleasure to see you too, Anna."

CHAPTER 47

I am David

Anna brings me into the library, and sitting just inside are four boxes, the four that I brought with me, that contain David's books.

"There is an empty bookcase that you can use and organize your books however you like. If you write the bookcase number just inside the front cover, then your books will always be returned here if someone takes them out," Anna says.

I smile and ask if she has a pen.

I am unpacking the third box, one classic at a time, scrawling the corresponding number, *62*, on the inside of each book jacket before stowing them side by side in their new home. I hear a familiar beat growing louder from the hallway. My heartbeat synchronizes to the *clip-clip* of her heels for a couple seconds, before gaining tempo and racing ahead to meet her at the doorway.

I try to stay focused on what I'm doing, or at least *seem* as though I am, when she enters the room.

"Hello, David, I'm Cassie," she says and I swallow her voice like neat liquor, traveling hot, right past my pounding heart and down to my stomach.

The book in my hand trembles, and I have to put in down before it gives me away. "Hi, I'm David." My words flounder and fall to the floor.

I'm embarrassed at having introduced myself after she addressed me by name. "I guess you already know that, sorry, I'm ... " I stand up and turn to face her. "Nice to meet you."

There is a smile waiting behind her expression. "Anna tells me that you brought your own library."

"My books mean a lot to me; no matter where you are, you can always go back to the places you have loved in books," I say.

"Do you mind if I look through them?" she asks.

"No, not at all, go right ahead." I stand there like a child holding up a stick figure drawing, waiting for approval.

"*The Time Machine.*" She pulls the book out. "I haven't read this since I was a little girl."

I have to hold my tongue. *I knew you would love them, Cassie.*

"I'm a sucker for classic science fiction," I say.

"Me too. I can't believe it; you have so many of my favorite books here," she says and stares in awe.

I try not to stare, but I can't help it. My view of her is no longer static, and I strafe a little to my right to see the light pinstripe the curve of her cheek. It's as though both mere seconds and an eternity have been and gone since we were together in the same room. I have loved her for so long that I am unsure if I can ever pretend otherwise.

My heart beats a complex irregular rhythm. I find myself lost in her image as it softens and is replaced by dissipating spots of light. I stagger back before reaching a hand for the arm of a chair, slowly sinking to a crouch. I feel my body slump to the carpet as everything goes dark. My broken heart skips and kicks my chest, digging a heel into the back of my sternum.

"David?" Her hand touches my neck and my wrist.

'David, can you hear me?" she says from somewhere far away.

CHAPTER 48

I am transparent

"Cass must have made quite an impression on you," Anna says.

"Why do you say that?" I say and continue to swallow the pills one-by-one as I sip the water.

"You were calling for her in your sleep," she says.

"Really?" As I wince, so does my heart, and with it comes a stabbing pain that makes me wonder if, in my condition, it is actually possible to die from embarrassment.

"You've been confined to bed rest for a few days, David," Anna says.

"What happened?" I ask.

"The doctor says that you are putting too much strain on your heart and that you have to take it easy for a little while," she says, "No more lifting boxes or chasing after nurses in your sleep."

I smile and the first few notes of a laugh escape my throat without permission. "I was looking forward to exploring the house," I say.

"If you are feeling better after I've finished my rounds, then I will take you for a tour," she says and gestures to the wheelchair in the corner of my room.

"Oh, it's okay, Anna, I don't want to be a burden," I say.

"Not at all, David. This is not a hospital; it's your home," she says.

"Thank you, Anna," I say as she leaves my room with a smile.

I pick up my book, continuing from where I left off, and soon, I am fleeing across the fringes with David, Rosalind, and Petra, fully immersed in their efforts to escape.

***

My own escape is interrupted when I realize that Anna is standing in my doorway. "Sorry, did you say something?" I ask.

"Are you ready for your tour?"

I put my book down and slowly swing my legs down off the bed. Anna rushes to help me, and I tell her I'm okay, but she ignores this and escorts me to the wheelchair, supporting some of my weight as she helps lower me into it.

I am reminded of our past rituals. "I'm really sorry, Anna."

"For what?" she asks.

"All of the special treatment and extra work for you; I don't want to put anyone out," I say.

"Doctor's orders, David; no physical stress. It's not your fault, and you're not putting me out," she says and unfolds a thick blanket to cover my legs.

"I really appreciate it, Anna," I say, but what I mean is, I appreciate everything that she has done for me my whole life.

"I do this because I like to help people, David; it's not a chore." She smiles as she tucks the blanket out of the way of the wheels.

"You're a Saint." I look her in the eyes, hoping that she will recognize her adoring nephew behind David's eyes.

"No, my mother was a Saint," she says and moves around to the back of the chair.

"She must be very proud of you, Anna," I say.

My thoughts turn to my own parents. I will never be able to talk to them again as their son. To them, I died and hopefully moved on to a better place. I did not ascend or descend but instead moved horizontally into the life of another, merely changing camera angle from static to mobile. The thought of leaving my parents behind and not being able to tell them that I am okay saddens me in a way far more tangible than the vicarious loss of David's mother had, but I am no longer Daniel Stockholm, and neither am I David Wolfe. I am simply a ghost with unfinished business.

***

Anna pushes me in the wheelchair, and I instinctively close my eyes as we exit the room, listening to the familiar *clip-slap* of her flat shoes. I open them again when Anna says, "This is C wing, our special care wing."

"Special care?" I ask peering through the open doors as we pass.

"Some of the residents require special help with cleaning or feeding," she says, "and there are some that are completely incapacitated."

"Coma?" I ask, in spite of my better instinct.

"Awake-unresponsive or persistent vegetative state patients," she says.

My stomach churns as her words summon memories of being trapped. Claustrophobia begins to set in, and my knuckles are bone white, gripped tight around the arms of the chair.

"I was in a coma," I say, "It was terrifying, being trapped and unable to ask for help."

Anna says nothing but continues to push me down the length of hallway C. Through an open door, I get a brief glimpse of a figure in a chair by the window, surrounded by machines. In the next room, there is a woman rocking in a wheelchair in front of the television, and I have to close my eyes again to the visual triggers to sickening nostalgia.

"This is the second dayroom, just for residents that require constant or regular help; this wing is not off limits to other residents, but it makes it easier on staff if those not needing full-time care use the other dayroom," she says.

I keep my eyes shut tight until a cool breeze strokes my face to let me know it is safe, and we exit through humming automatic double-doors to the gardens outside. I succumb to the calming effects of nature as we move slowly around the winding path that cuts through grass, trees, and flowerbeds. The grounds are large and surrounded by tall thick trees that square off the garden at the far end.

We enter the building at the other end. "This is the cafeteria. If you would rather take your meals in here than in your room, then just let us know."

We go through another corridor that leads us back into the library.

"Where are A and B wings?" I say.

"A and B are on the second floor; most of the residents of A and B are bedridden and in the final stages of their illness," she says.

Death row. I have no wish to continue my tour of the upstairs and foresee that I will be less than enthusiastic about my inevitable transition, when it finally comes.

We come to a stop back in my room, and I am mentally exhausted. Anna helps me out of the chair, and I don't resist the help.

"Thank you for the tour, Anna," I say.

"You're welcome, David; if you need anything else, then push the white button, and someone will come by as soon as they can. Don't push the red button unless it is a medical emergency," she says and smiles before exiting my room.

I let my slippers fall to the floor as I slide my legs under the covers and lay my head on my pillow. I can't get the images of C wing out of my mind. The feelings of being trapped, that have now become more than just far away memories, stir in my stomach. For the first time, I share the irrational fear of contagion with the countless voyeurs in Danny's past, recoiling from the clay-sculpted remnants of a tapeworm's entrée.

CHAPTER 49

I am the cowardly liar

I am walking steadfast to wing C. I don't know if it is morbid curiosity that is propelling me, or a need to conquer the almost crippling fear that gripped me previously, during my tour with Anna.

Beyond the first open door I come to, sits a boy with a blank and detached expression, surrounded by machines, some of which I recognize. My throat tightens, and my lower eyelids tremble as they fill with hot stinging tears. There is a clipboard hanging next to the ventilator, and I read the name aloud, "William Emerson."

"Hi, William, I'm David," I say as I wipe my eyes.

William maintains his posture and continues to stare forward. I attempt to speak again, but no words come out, only a whimpering, blubbering accompaniment to the streaming and uncontrollable tears.

***

As I make my cowardly retreat back to hallway D, I am plagued by memories of McGuire, of young David slouched down behind a car, hiding and drenched in self-pity, and seething with subsequent self-loathing.

When I get back to my room, I am crying and unable to stop. A million thoughts run through my mind at a confusing pace, and all of which leave me in a cold panic. Empathy for William and the frigid fear of my own fragility work like alternating pistons behind my tear ducts, as I sink down into my chair.

Prominent in my mind is the selfish and unrelenting realization that I have willingly entered the grim reaper's halfway house. My continued existence is nothing more than gloating arrogance, rubbed in the face of death as it lurks outside my periphery, waiting for the right time to reclaim its elusive quarry.

I do what I can to take my mind elsewhere. With my laptop open on the table, I scroll through countless photographs of strangers until I find the only face among them that means anything to me. Harry's words echo in my mind, "I am very proud of you, David." If he could see me now, would he still feel proud, or would he see me for the lying coward that I am, pleading before his image for the lending of courage.

CHAPTER 50

I am intrepid

I open the web browser, copy and enter the password given to me for the wireless Internet connection when prompted, and the Statham House home page opens with terms and conditions of use. I click agree without reading the above text and stare at the page, with William's face seemingly super imposed, as I type his name into the search bar at the top of my screen.

After scrolling through multiple social media profiles, looking for the boy in the chair, I almost dismiss his profile along with the rest bearing the same name, because the boy in the photo looks so different, the graven image seemingly more animated than its physical counterpart.

"Comment has been removed or deleted by user" underlines almost every other comment within each of the turn-based conversations. I browse through his photos, and there are pictures of William with other members of the chess club that bring similar images from David's unpopular childhood to the forefront of my mind. I see, "*Stranger in a Strange Land*," listed as one of his favorite books along with around ten or so other titles that are now on the shelves of bookcase sixty-two.

***

Almost two hours have passed before my return to room 157C, William's room. I hesitate at the doorway before walking in and sitting down in the chair. William's position and expression remain unchanged.

"I'm sorry I left in a hurry earlier, William," I say, "I'm new here, and I don't really know anyone. I was hoping that maybe we could be friends." My eyes well up again, and I take a second to compose myself.

"I brought a book along with me. I thought that maybe I could read it to you." I wipe the tears from my eyes and search for the courage to look into his. He is the picture of frozen innocence, a child locked in a daydream.

"*Stranger in a Strange Land* by Robert A. Heinlein," I say and open the book.

CHAPTER 51

I am the scarecrow

Last night there was a crow outside my window, cawing and keeping me awake into the early hours of the morning. When sleep finally came, the crow came along with it, infiltrating my subconscious, whispering the synopsis of a dream-memory hybrid of my family's last trip to Africa.

We were housed in large tents and kept inside the compound for most of the trip because of escalating violence in and around the neighboring villages. There were armed militia in the streets, and the sound of distant gunfire played like tribal drumming in the background of every conversation.

We were allowed to leave the compound on the condition of strict adhesion to specific routes and with the accompaniment of an armed escort. I made a comment to my mother about the dead crows that were strewn along our route and in the villages. My mother's reaction to my comment was a worried glance that begged for silence, adding to the tension in the vehicle, which seemed to have replaced the hot air around us.

I was told to remain in the back seat of the guarded jeep while my mother haggled for supplies within the village. I am not sure if the armed guards were appointed by government or paid for by the church, or by my parents, but at least one remained with each of us at all times.

Through the window of the Jeep, I watched as villagers scattered and disappeared into houses as the militia came through firing shots into the air and dragging people into their trucks. They pulled three children from a house, in a tug-of-war fashion, with their hysterical parents dragging behind them like the entrails of a mortally wounded animal. As the children were loaded into the truck, the mother and father were made to kneel at gunpoint as one of the armed men set fire to their house. A crow cawed from the roof of the family's home as it began to smolder and smoke. The muzzle of the semi-automatic rifle was raised from the father's forehead to the roof of their home, and a round was pumped into the black bird before it rolled and fell next to the crying couple.

Later that day, within the safety of the compound, I overheard my parents in one of the tents talking with their translator. He was asking my parents to consider abandoning the construction, or at least putting the project on hold, because of the escalating hostility. My parents were adamant about staying for the completion of the medical depository, but agreed to stay within the compound for the remainder of their visit.

The translator had also asked for more stringent treatment of food waste within the compound as it was attracting crows. My mother asked about the significance of the crows, and why there were hundreds of the dead birds littering the streets in and around the village, and his reply was that the crow was a bad omen, thought by some, to be a spy for the witches. He said that the militia kill them as a warning to witches, and the villagers kill any around their homes that would be interpreted by militia as a sign of witchcraft in the house. People used to see the crows as guides for the soul, a blessing, but the villagers have come to see them now as a bad omen, a harbinger of death.

The crows were perched on the high walls of the compound, cawing and waiting for food scraps. I was terrified that the crows would bring the militia back to our camp. I spent the next few hours running around, shouting, chasing, and throwing rocks at the crows. I winged a few, which made the rest caw louder. I didn't want to kill the birds, but I wanted them gone before the militia returned.

***

I woke up this morning in a cold sweat, with the loud cawing chorus still echoing in my mind as I sat up.

The lingering fear from my dream still wraps my thoughts as I question if the crow outside my window last night was indeed a spy for the underworld, sent by death to search me out.

CHAPTER 52

I am the antecedent

I have with me the box of items that I had requested, and that Harry brought for me during his visit this morning. I set them down on the table in 157-C; William sits still in the same position he's been in every time that I have visited him.

"This may be a little more interesting than the boring white walls," I say as I unroll the massive poster of the Orion nebula and pin it to the wall. I show him the items as I pull them from the box. Every movie listed on his profile under favorites. Complete box sets of his favorite television shows, mostly science fiction.

"And I brought a chess set for when you get better," I say and sit down in the chair with the book I've been reading to him. I open it to chapter nineteen.

After three or four pages, I look up and there's a large man standing in the doorway. I close the book and stand. "Sorry, I didn't see you there."

"Who are you?" he says, which comes across like, *name and rank?*

"David, room 117-D," I say with a dither.

"George Emerson." He extends a hand that looks more like a baseball mitt as it wraps around mine.

"You're William's father?" I ask, as I'm shook by the hand.

He nods. "Where did all of this stuff come from?"

I feel a sudden guilt for having encroached without permission. "I had it brought in for William. I'm sorry, I should have asked if it was alright," I say, mentally squirming for adequate reason.

"What's this?" he asks, pointing at the poster.

"It's a photo of the Orion nebula, taken by the Hubble telescope," I say, "I thought it would be better than the plain white walls."

"Will loved this stuff." George stares in the direction of the poster but seems to be looking right through it, and the wall.

I don't say anything.

"I always wanted him to get into sports. I never took any interest in any of this stuff," he says and closes his eyes.

I try to stay the feelings of claustrophobia, stemming from the fact that this large man is standing directly in the way of the room's only exit.

"I was an athlete all the way through high school and college; I thought he'd take after me. I signed him up for everything, but he wasn't interested in any of it, would rather play chess, or read a book," he says and turns a stern gaze toward me.

"Why did you bring all this stuff in here?" George's eyes narrow, and for a second, I am reminded of the fear I felt, standing in McGuire's shadow with nowhere to run.

Backed into a corner, I am a Wolfe with a demeanor more fitting of a startled rabbit. "I was in a coma ... " I start, "I could hear everyone around me talking, sometimes I could even see what was going on, but I was trapped inside, and I couldn't do anything about it. If William is aware of what is going on around him, then we should make him as comfortable as we can."

George reaches out, and I flinch inside, but he reaches past me and takes the book. "*Stranger in a Strange Land?*"

"He has it listed as one of his favorites on his profile," I say as I shuffle my toes inside my slippers.

"His profile?" he says, turning the book over.

"I looked him up online; I was just trying to help ... "

"You think he can hear us?" he says and there is a pleading look behind the wet glass of his eyes.

"I know that I would rather waste my time reading to him, even if he *can't* hear me, than leave him staring at a plain white wall and alone with the chance that he *can*," I say, careful not to let my tone come across as chastising.

"Do you know what happened to my son?" His harsh tone cracks a little, and I watch the hair on his thick forearms stand up from the flesh as it goose bumps.

I shake my head. "No, I don't."

He stares right through me, and I don't know where to look.

"All the jock kids at his school, they pushed him around, bullied him, and beat him. He hid it from his mother and me, or we ignored it, I don't know. All the sports and bullshit I signed him up for, just put him right there, with all of those guys. I let them have him. Will said in his note that it had been going on for years, and he couldn't take it anymore; he couldn't get away from them, and he could never be like me." Tears roll down his cheeks, and I can almost see the mechanical refocusing of his eyes back on mine.

"He hung himself with his goddamn school tie," he growls, and he begins to shake, trying to hold it in. His hands are trembling; his mouth is twitching and quivering.

"He was my boy, my son, and those fucking kids ... " he starts and wipes the tears from his eyes, "I was one of those kids when I was in school. I picked on the nerds, the losers, the geeks, and God is paying me back. It might as well have been me that bullied and beat him. He did nothing to anyone. He was my son, he was innocent, and I did it, I killed him." He looks at William and drops to his knees. "I'm so sorry. I'm sorry I gave you to those animals; I'm sorry I didn't listen."

George is crying into the lap of his son's statue for minutes before he remembers, or cares, that I'm still in the room. He wipes his face and tries to compose himself, and I don't know what to say, or if there is anything I *can* say.

"So this is his favorite?" he says, choking on his words and swallowing to force whatever tears are left, back inside, as he picks up the book from the floor.

"Yes," I say. Part of me wants to tell him that I was bullied, and that I know some of what William must have gone through, but this would do nothing, if not twist the knife that has already inflicted a fatal wound.

"Where did you get up to?" he says and sits down in the chair.

"Chapter nineteen," I say.

He flicks through the pages, stopping at the bookmarked page and begins to read. I leave the room quietly and listen as George's voice starts like an old car during winter, before regaining its previous goliath stature.

CHAPTER 53

I am behind the curtain

I exit through the cafeteria and hold the door open for myself as I leave David's statue to wait as a patient doorman, while I move freely through the gardens and the facility.

The gardens are beautiful pinks, purples, and oranges and stand out brightly against the blue-black sky above. I stroll slowly around the path and lie down on the bed of nails where the grass used to be, staring up into the black, looking for frozen yellow spies.

I take my time on the way back and enter through the door held open graciously by my former self. I wander through the cafeteria and around the library for a while, looking at the raised lettering of old books and trying to read the names of any book that still has the fresh fingerprints of life on its spine.

I pass my room and make my way to the lights in the open expanse of the dayroom. There are more lights than residents, and as I get closer, I realize that some of the lights are without the dark body outlines that contain the majority about the room. By the relation in shape and size, I determine that two of the lights in a large group are Cassie and Anna. When I am close enough to make out Cassie's features, I see that all but a few of the group around them are without body. Of the bodiless entourage surrounding them both, there stands a small, lighted figure by Anna's side that appears to be holding her hand.

CHAPTER 54

I am serendipitous

I want nothing more than to talk to Cassie, but I have been waiting for the right time to strike up conversation, or perhaps, waiting for fate to step in, all the while, hoping that death's tendency for procrastination is more prevalent than my own. I imagine future conversations with Cassie and yearn for her to hold my hand in hers, now that I am able to appreciate the gift of her touch. I know that the relationship, in whatever capacity, between Cassie and I must develop naturally, organically, or I will run the risk of becoming an unwanted nuisance or pest. I will bide my time, even though it is the very commodity that I am most limited in.

***

I have kept myself occupied for the most part, either in the library or in William's room. George had asked if I would continue to read to his son between visiting hours, and I told him that I would be happy to, and have honored his request daily, today being of no exception.

***

I put the book down on the table after securing the bookmark between the pages, and I notice that William is no longer staring straight forward, but at the poster on his wall. Only his eyes have moved, and I second-guess myself, questioning if he has moved at all, then his eyes loll down to his right.

SKIN CAGE

I pull my chair to in front of his. "William, can you look at my left hand?" I hold both of my hands up in front of me.

His eyes remain pointed down and to his right.

"Can you look at my right hand?" I ask and flick my eyes from his, to the target hand.

His eyes move slowly up, past my hand, to the corner of the room.

"Now my left again?" I say.

His eyes drop once more to his right and down.

"Can you blink for me?" I ask, but he remains still.

"That's okay; can you look left, right, and back to let me know that you can hear me?" I say, my excitement causing my voice to shake.

Slowly his eyes travel from bottom right to top left, and back and forth.

"I'll be right back, William," I call, as I turn and run out of the room to find Cassie.

I happen upon Anna first, "Where's Cassie?"

"She's up on the second floor, what do need?" she says, flinching as she turns to face me.

"Can you get her to come down here and meet me in William's room?" I say, bouncing with nervous energy.

She doesn't have a chance to respond.

"Please, Anna, it's important, 157-C," I say.

"What ... "

"It's urgent, she needs to see," I say, cutting her off.

"Okay, David, calm down, I will get her for you." She motions her hands like a pianist and waves them up and down a fraction.

I hurry back to William's room and explain to him that I want him to do the same thing for Cassie when she gets here, and I continue to test him, afraid that if I stop, he will recoil once again to the back of his cage.

I hear Cassie's heels, *clipping* quickly in the hallway, followed by what I assume is Anna, a few seconds later.

"What's going on, what's wrong?" Cassie says through panting breaths.

"Watch," I say, "Look left for me," and William complies.

"Look right," I say, and he does. "Look left."

I turn to Cassie. "He can *hear* us."

She kneels in front of William and repeats the process through a beaming smile.

I'm shaking, and there is a pain shooting down my leg. Not wanting to detract attention from William, I move through the door and out into the hallway to calm down. The wall and floor turn and narrow. I feel a dull thud against my head as the wall moves to catch my fall. The hallway spins, and I collapse facing the dimming lights. I can hear Anna's voice, calling for Cassie.

CHAPTER 55

I am the tin man

"David?"

After opening my eyes, it takes a short while for me to focus and reorganize the blur of a large figure, standing in the doorway to my room.

"George?"

"I want to thank you for what you did for Will," he says as he enters and comes to stand next to my bed.

"What I did?" I ask, rubbing the sleep from my eyes.

"They've got him hooked up to a computer; he's talking," he says.

I sit up, "Really?"

"Take it easy; Anna told me not to get you excited, or she'll see to it that I end up in worse shape than you," he says, smiling.

I chuckle at the thought of Aunt Anna chastising George and ask, "So what did William say?"

"He likes the poster," George says, "He asked me to thank you for reading to him, and for being his friend."

"Tell him he's welcome, and I'll come to see him as soon as I'm allowed to leave my room. I've been relegated to bed rest for the rest of the week," I say and wait for George to respond, as he searches the floor of my room for words that are somehow lost, within the reflected light from my window.

"They told me you were running around to get the nurse for Will, that's why you collapsed," he says in a more somber tone.

"I've got a bad heart; I'm supposed to take it easy, or so they keep telling me," I say, in a way that makes my condition sound more like a chore than a death sentence.

"Is there anything I can do for you?" he asks.

"No, I'm okay, they're looking after me," I say, "Anna's been walking me around the gardens every day."

"You and Nurse Mathews gave me my son back; I don't know how to repay you for that, but if there's anything you need," he says.

"I have everything I need, George," I say and offer thanks, by way of a smile.

"Well, if you think of anything," he says, and I know that I will have to think of something eventually, if only for the purpose of allowing a strong man the opportunity of repaying a debt to his pride.

"George?" I call, as he's about to leave.

He turns and raises his eyebrows.

"You should ask them to hook a printer up to Will's computer and set it up so that he can print what he writes. It would be nice for him to be able to say whatever he wants, and not have to wait for an audience," I say.

He nods and smiles. "That's a good idea. I'll tell Nurse Mathews. Thanks, David, for everything."

After George leaves, I try to fall back asleep, but the room is bright, and I'm as well rested as a man can possibly be. I read for a while to pass the time until Anna comes to get me for my walk. She insists that I let her help me into the chair and covers me with a thick blue blanket that makes me feel more decrepit. She takes me the long way through the facility, and as we are just nearing the exit doors, I hear Cassie call, "Anna?"

We stop and Cassie comes around to the side of the wheelchair to face us both.

"What is it, Cass?" Anna says.

"I was hoping to talk to David," Cassie says, and my heart jumps.

"I was just about to take him for a walk in the gardens; you can take over if you like, dear," Anna says.

Cassie glances at me, "Is that okay, David?"

I try for an indifferent smile and stammer a response. "That's fine with me."

"Great, thanks, Anna." Cassie pushes the button to open the doors and moves behind me. I close my eyes and breathe her in before the breeze from outside steals the sweet and intoxicating smell of her skin away from me.

"It's a little cool outside; would you like another blanket or anything, David?" she asks as we exit the building.

"I'm okay, thank you, Cassie." The minor sufferance of cool air whistling past my sock-less ankles is a small price to pay for the chance to be alone with the woman I adore.

We come to a stop next to a bench, and she takes a seat. "We haven't really had the chance to sit and get to know one another yet."

"I know, my heart keeps getting in the way." I smirk.

She smiles, and it's everything I can do to keep my heart from racing.

"You have a big heart, David," she says.

"It's just swollen," I say breathing a laugh through my nose.

"That's not what I meant; that was a wonderful thing that you did for William," she says and looks me in the eyes.

I am lost for a second in her beautiful brown eyes, and I yearn to hold her.

"George says you've got him hooked up to a computer, and he's talking," I say, blinking myself out of a trance.

"He's been asking about you, David, he wanted to know if you were okay. I told him that you're doing fine, but you have to take it easy for a little while," she says.

Cassie looks back toward the building. "He's been in the dayroom all morning watching back-to-back *Star Trek* episodes from the box set you brought for him."

"I'm glad he likes them." I follow her gaze to the house, and my mouth forms into a wide smile on its own.

"He told me to tell you that he forgives you for 'creeping his profile' too," she says.

I let out a brief chuckle. "I can't wait to speak with him."

"He's doing really well for an HAI patient," she says.

"HAI?"

"Sorry, Hypoxic-anoxic injury. Depriving the brain of oxygen," she says, and her mind seems to be elsewhere.

"George told me what happened, why he's here I mean," I say.

Cassie looks down into her lap. "It was terrible what happened to William, and what his parents must have gone through."

We sit in silence for a moment, both of us watching her hands move nervously around imaginary soap.

"Before I came back here, to this facility, I looked after an unresponsive boy; well, he wasn't a boy at the end, but he was about William's age when I first began care," she says.

I watch her stop and start to speak a few times, searching for what she wants to say.

"His name was Daniel Stockholm; I grew very attached to him. You can't help but give a little of your heart to someone after nine years of caring for them like one of your own family," she says, and I can see the emotion welling up in her.

I search for a way for *David* to contribute to the conversation. "I read about Daniel Stockholm in the newspaper."

We trade glances, and after a second, she says, "We tried the eye tracking thing with Danny too, but it didn't work. I wanted so much for him to be able to talk to me."

"I'm sorry that it didn't work; that must have been hard on everyone," I say, and I remember it like it was yesterday.

"I don't know if he could hear me, or if he even knew I was there," she says.

"He could hear you, Cassie," I say without thinking, and Cassie looks up at me. I take a second. "You have to hope, right?"

She nods. "Hope is all you've got sometimes."

"What's going to happen to the other care worker, Salt?" I ask, feigning effort to remember his name.

"Marcus? He's been committed to ongoing psychiatric evaluation," she says.

"So he's not going to jail?" I ask.

"No, it doesn't look like it, but he's going to be in the mental facility for a few years, while he gets the help he needs," she says.

Hearing the news that Marcus is not going to be sentenced to a lifetime in jail helps relieve a small portion of the guilt. "Anna worked there too, right?"

"Danny was her nephew," she says, nodding slowly.

"How is she holding up?" I ask.

"Anna's strong. She says that she thinks Danny is in a better place." Cassie smiles, but her eyes wince a little as she says it.

"I think that she's right," I say and return her smile, "I figured that you would have to believe in some kind of afterlife, in your line of work."

"It helps to have faith, or at the very least, hope," she says and glances down at her watch, "I had better get you back inside."

I nod in response, and as she stands, she says, "I just wanted to say thank you, David, for what you did for William."

"Thank *you*, Cassie, for keeping my heart beating," I say.

"Well, actually it's the medication that is doing *that*, not me," she says.

My heart has beat only for her, for as long as I have loved her, and it feels like I have loved her for an eternity. I don't tell her this. I just smile.

CHAPTER 56

I am in check

You might as well give up, David is the message on the screen.
"I'm just rusty," I say, and I'm trying desperately to recall David's memory of chess tactics.
I move the queen in a desperate, last-ditch effort to save myself, and as soon as I take my fingers off of the piece and look up, I see that William has already written his next move on the screen, followed by *checkmate*.
"Wow." I shake my head. "That's enough for me, I admit defeat."
Are you sure? You need the practice.
"Yes, I'm sure. I guess I'm not as good at chess as I remember," I say.
Nurse Cassie says that they are coming today to modify the software so I can use the Internet and check my email.
"That's great. I'll ask if we can download some e-books and audio books to your computer, if you want," I say.
I like it when you and my dad read to me.
"I'll still read to you, but if you wake up early and you're bored, you'll have something to help pass the time," I say.
How is your heart?
"I'm okay. I just have to stay calm and relaxed," I say.
Like, Bruce Banner.
"Bruce Banner?" I ask.
When he gets angry or excited, he turns green, starts smashing stuff?
I laugh. "Yeah, only I turn bright red and fall down."
The screen remains blank. I look back to William. "Sorry, I'm okay. I'm feeling a lot better, Will."
Are you going to die?

I look around the room, stalling for the right answer to come to me, and when I return my attention to the screen, another question mark appears, and I relent with a nod. "I don't know how long I have left, Will."

What do you think happens after we die?

"I don't know, but I'm certain that we go on, after we leave our bodies," I say.

You mean like a soul?

"Yeah, I guess so," I say.

What do you want to do before you die?

"Beat you at chess," I say through a smirk.

You want me to let you win?

"I was just going easy on you, but now it's on," I say and reset the pieces on the board, "Best four of seven?"

CHAPTER 57

I am evanescing

"This is Harry and Barb," I say gesturing to each.

"Hi, I'm Cassie," she says smiling, "I've heard a lot about you two over the last while."

"Likewise," says Barb with a smile, "I'm glad David's got someone in here looking after him."

Anna appears at the door and says something to Cassie in a hushed tone, Cassie nods, and I catch, "Okay, I'll be there in a couple minutes."

"It was nice to finally meet you both, but I'm afraid I've got to run," Cassie says with an apologetic smile.

"Nice meeting you," Harry says.

"Bye, Cassie," Barb adds.

I wait for Cassie to leave. "So did you bring the cake with the file in it?"

Barb smiles, and Harry asks, "How are you holding up?"

"I'm okay. I'm just tired, even though all I seem to do is sleep. I'm not supposed to be over-exerting myself," I say.

"Is there anything that you want us to bring for you, next time we come?" Barb asks and touches my hand.

"There's nothing I need." I smile. "I'm glad you guys came, that's all I want."

"Barb said she was going to sneak a bottle of wine in here for us," Harry says chuckling.

"Really?"

Barb smiles. "I thought about it, but I don't want to get you in trouble with your nurse."

"Remember the kid you brought the box of movies and stuff for, William?" I say.

Harry nods.

"He's moving around and talking," I say, "Actually speaking, not through the computer."

"Really? That's great," Harry says.

"Who's William?" Barb asks, and we take a few minutes to fill her in on the details.

"Looks like he's going to be getting out of here pretty soon and going back home," I say.

"That's great, good for him," Harry says.

"So, Cassie seems nice," Barb says, and she's smiling at me.

"What's with the smile?" I say with a smirk of my own.

Harry looks back and forth. "Did I miss something?"

"David's nurse," Barb says.

"Oh, yes, she seems like a nice girl," he says, still seemingly missing what Barb is driving at.

"She's an angel," I say, "Actually, all the staff here are great."

"Not all as cute as that one though," Barb says raising one eyebrow.

"Trying to *start* a relationship with a broken heart doesn't really seem like a good idea," I say, "besides, if she looked at me sideways, I would have a heart attack."

"You'd make a cute couple though," Barb says.

"Alright, quit teasing. What about Brad and the kids; you get started on that yet?" I say.

"I hired a relief manager to watch the bar while I'm in Paris," she says with the widest smile that her face can handle.

"Really? When are you going?" I say, and I feel a twinge in my chest, but make every effort not to show it.

"The end of this month, if all goes well." Her expression flashes with excitement.

"I'm really happy for you, Barb, you'll have a great time," I say and try to stifle an uncontrollable yawn, "Sorry."

As I am rubbing the wet from my eyes, Harry stands up. "We'd better get going and let you get your rest, David."

I want to protest, but I'm having trouble keeping my eyes open. "Alright, I'll see you soon, Harry."

"Bye, David," Barb says.

"Bye, Barb."

CHAPTER 58

I am the moth

I managed to wheel myself down to Will's room earlier today. It is hard to imagine that the excitable teenager wheeling around room 157C appeared outwardly, as nothing more than an angelic statuesque surrogate only months before. We played what could possibly be our last game of chess, and I finally beat him. I joked that I thought he was cheating before, that it was really the computer playing, which made him laugh.

He told me that he would be leaving the facility tomorrow afternoon. As he did so, a wide range of emotion could be seen welling up just below the translucent surface, attributed perhaps to the joy of being able to return home, while at the same time, having to leave his new friends behind.

I am almost certain that the single tear, which was allowed to escape, was driven by the very same reason that drove him to let me win at chess. I understand now, why David made every effort to cut himself off from anyone who would be left to mourn his passing.

I fell asleep in the wheelchair on my way back from Will's room. I vaguely remember Anna pushing me the rest of the way, and helping me into bed, still only half-awake. The frequent shooting pains down my arms and legs are near unbearable now, and the headaches are back with increasing intensity.

Cassie has stopped in on me every day, and I try to stay awake while she is with me, but I'm so exhausted. I'm beginning to wonder when they will move me upstairs.

***

There is a pressure roughly centered on my chest that hones to a sharp point and sinks slowly through my heart. Chemical fire flows through my arms and legs, and my head is pounding, synchronized to the elevated beat of my heart, the percussive accompaniment to my slow, painful evacuation. I reach out a trembling hand to hit the red button.

The pain is at once gone, and with it, the brightness and color of the room fade to dark blue. I stand from my bed and turn to see David's body lying there, still glowing a faint green. Apocalyptic fire rages within his chest with no apparent regard for collateral damage. I reach out to touch his chest, and it is unrelenting, solid, turned to stone.

This cannot be how it ends. I have so much to tell her, although I will never be able to tell her who I am, and how much I love her. I just want to say goodbye.

I can hear something in the distance, but I'm not sure if it is actually sound. I move out into the hallway, and it seems louder, clearer, and I continue toward it. The usual glowing figures populate the hallway, but something seems different, and as I pass through the dayroom, I realize what it is. The figures are moving at a slow, almost imperceptible speed, but they are moving.

The sound or feeling beckons me, and I follow it to the stairwell door, ignoring thoughts of a hooded skeletal figure, sitting in wait on the stairs. I turn back as I grip the door handle to view the quickened pace of the figures in the hallway, confirming my assertion of movement. I apply great pressure to the door, and it opens slowly into the stairwell, steadily resisting my efforts like the outer door of a fully submerged, shipwrecked vessel.

I reach the landing at the top of the stairs and pull at the door to the second floor with both hands. It gives easier than the last and opens to a floodlit room. The bright blue-green light grows brighter at the far end of the room. Passing figures slow down to regard me as they move toward the slowly spinning light.

Small wisps of light float as though carried by a current, bringing with them a memory from my childhood. The extra cobweb-like material, used to make the flights of a hunter's dart, given back to the earth with a single breath across an open palm, the seeds dispersing, floating on the breeze and glowing in the afternoon sunlight. I can almost feel the warmth of that afternoon sun on my face. It feels like home, an unconditional loving embrace.

As I follow the lights, I am slowed by something, as though once again submerged along with the shipwrecked vessel. Conflicting magnetic forces push and pull at me until I relent, turning away from the eternal loving light, its attraction vanquished by the love I have for her, for Cassie.

I turn, swing open the door, and run down the stairs, although I am not sure if my feet actually touch the ground. I wrench open the door, and the bright-lit figures spin toward me as I enter the hallway, their collective attention remaining fixed on the door as I move swiftly between them.

The figures are moving with regular speed, and I can see lights crowding around the entrance to my room. I weave through the figures to get inside, to where Anna stands, accompanied by the same small glowing figure at her side, holding her hand. I slow to view the small figure as it raises a free hand, stretching out toward me. As I take her hand, I know her, as if we were one and the same.

Cassie stands next to the bed, leaning in over David's body, which is dark save for a small glowing vapor at its center. I am begging God to let me in, to give me the chance to say goodbye to her. I climb the foot of the bed and turn as I fall toward him, giving myself completely to a singular desire. There is a brief flash, and my body reacts to inertia, like waking up from a dream of falling. There is light, noise, pain and panic, then silence, and blackness.

CHAPTER 59

I am talking to an angel

The image of the most beautiful angel imaginable dissolves the fog between us, and her Jersey Lily smile caresses my broken heart.

"David?" she says softly.

"Hi," I say returning her smile.

"We thought we'd lost you," she says and takes my hand in hers.

"I saw lights, Cassie."

"Lights?" she stands puzzled, with the hint of a tremulous smile, poised, waiting for the punch line.

I raise my head to view Anna. "I saw Adia. She's with you right now, holding your hand. She told me to tell you that she loves you, Anana."

"Anana? No one knows me by *that* name," Anna says, and for the first time in my life, I watch her cry.

"Who's Adia?" Cassie says.

"Adia means, 'the gift of life,' and it was the name of my sister," Anna says, wiping the tears from her face.

"David?" Cassie says.

"I have something to tell you both," I say and wait for both Cassie and Anna to look at me.

"Danny wants you both to know that he was always listening." I turn to Cassie. "When you told him stories about Brian from your childhood, when you read all of those wonderful books to him, he was listening and he loved them all. He wants you to know that he loves you both, with all of his soul, and that he will be with you always," I say.

Cassie's eyes begin to well up. She cups her hand to her mouth and speaks softly.

SKIN CAGE

"I can't believe it. It can't be true," she says.

"He was listening then, and he is listening now, Cassie," I say, gently squeezing her hand.

"How do I know that this isn't just some cruel joke?" Cassie says.

"People talk to God every day without knowing if anyone is truly listening; sometimes all you have is faith, or hope," I say.

"What if faith isn't enough?" she says.

"He asked if you would continue to read to him," I say, and hand her my copy of *The Chrysalids*, "from where you left off."

Tears fall from her autumn eyes as she reads the title. She looks all about the room, before the subtle beginnings of a laugh turn into whispered words, "Yes, I will read to you every day, Danny."

"I'm tired," I say, "Can you tell William that I said goodbye?"

Anna comes to Cassie's side, and both now stand arm in arm, looking down at me. As the room dissolves, the smiling faces of two loving angels remain, as a template for the most beautiful dream, and I close my heavy, tired eyes.

***

I am no longer afraid of death, and if I am permitted, I will forego heaven, or whatever awaits me in the afterlife, to hear Cassie's voice as she reads aloud each day, to the memory of Danny.

The end

Made in the USA
Charleston, SC
25 February 2015